I0732244

LAURIE BOULDEN

Mistress of Moab
Ruth's Story
Fruit of Her Hands Series

Laurie Boulden

Proverbs 31:31- Give her of the *fruit of her hands*; and let her own works praise her in the gates.

Remarkable women make for amazing stories. The valor with which they took hold of the situations in their lives induced incredible feats. God provided for each of them. Grace in time of struggle. Mercy in place of judgement and death. Love where love was needed.

Step back in time, sit around the fire, and listen to the storyteller. May the acts of courage evident in the lives of Rahab, Ruth, and Esther reflect in all of us

.

Introduction

Ruth is one of my favorite Old Testament stories. I admit, I'm a romantic. Who doesn't enjoy a good romance? That's exactly my vision for Ruth's story. Not only is it her romance with Boaz, it is also God's romance with us.

Naomi's family likely lived in Moab about fifteen years, at least ten of them without Elimelech. When Naomi brings Ruth to Bethlehem, the first of the spring feasts, Pesach, has just taken place. It would be forty-nine days to the wheat harvest, so seven weeks. That's the time we have for the events of our story to unfold. This is a love story, for Ruth and for us. The journey to write this story has been an interesting one. Enjoy the read. May you feel the love of God in its telling. Blessings.

Book 1: What Comes Before
Chapter Ehad (one)

"Ruth." Pottery shattered on the stone floor as the sound of an aging man screamed her name. Ruth hid in the corner of the upstairs room, behind the loom. A large opening let a breeze twirl through the sunlit space. Blue skies dotted with white billowing clouds soared above Moab. *What if I could soar like those clouds*? With her arms wrapped around her knees as she leaned against the rough-hewn wall, her heart thudded at the thought of leaping through the window to fly far, far away where Father could no longer…

Something moving in the distance disrupted her thoughts. Dust billowed across uneven land. Not animals, well, except for oxen pulling wagons. Three wagons. They couldn't be local. They were coming toward the house.

Father went to meet them, shaking hands with a tall, slender man who climbed down from the first wagon. Though she couldn't hear more than murmuring, Ruth watched as Father and the stranger waved their arms and gestured. The discussion went on for a while. Ruth's attention turned to the middle wagon where a boy held reins of the oxen. Another boy also controlled the third wagon. Both boys had yet to reach manhood. No hair darkened their faces. The first boy balanced himself standing up on the seat of the wagon. Ruth watched, expecting to see him fall. She wasn't disappointed.

A woman turned to glare at the boy. Though not a young woman, she gathered her skirts and jumped to the ground. The boy scrambled to regain his seat. Ruth could nether see the look nor hear the exchange, but the boy lowered his face. Was she angry? Would she strike? Or was that only a father's place? The next moment, the strange woman moved to the side, offered her hand to the boy, then held on as he jumped to the ground. She clapped. The other boy ran to them and she gave him a lesson in jumping off the wagon as well.

Father and the stranger reached some sort of agreement, because when the man moved toward the wagons, the woman shewed the boys to return to their positions then she went to join him. She remained a step behind, as was proper, but shaded her eyes to look at Father, then at the house. Father pointed toward the region where the sun would set, and they both turned. Something in Ruth longed to see them all up close. She clambered down the wood ladder to the main courtyard of the house, hurried through the open gate, and around the animal shade. She stopped beside a gnarled olive tree trunk, rubbing her hand against its rough bark. Father didn't seem to notice her. She took a few steps closer.

The woman saw her first. Her sweet face smiled at Ruth. She wasn't too different. Her skin was darker, and her hair was thick and deeper black than her own brownish-red mop. Ruth gave a tiny smile in return.

"Ruth."

She jumped at the sound of her name, then quickly turned to Father.

His brows furrowed, but he showed no other sign of ill humor. "We will have guests with our meal. Prepare for them. The lads can eat out here with the animals."

The woman leaned closer to the man and said something. He put his hand forward for a favor. "My wife, Naomi, asks permission to help your daughter. She wishes to see how the hearthstone and kitchen work in your house. If you permit."

Father blinked, then smiled. "Of course. The peace of our Fathers be upon you." He turned and walked away. The man went to assist the boys, and Ruth looked at the woman in awe.

She smiled again. "It is well?"

Ruth nodded. "I have chickens in the back." She took a path around the side of the house. Naomi followed. Between them they caught two birds. With help, it did not take long to dress them.

Ruth pulled the stone from the fire and stoked the coals until little flames licked at the fresh fuel.

Naomi cut yams to add to the chicken. "Where is your mother?"

"She died when I was a baby."

"YHWY bless you, child. How old are you now?"

"Fourteen, I think. Father does not always remember the feast of years."

"I am not familiar with that festival."

"It is after the harvest. We celebrate life and bounty. There are sixteen years to the threshold. Each year we get to move once step closer."

"What happens at the threshold?"

Ruth tilted her head. "I don't know."

Naomi laughed. "You are still young. I suppose you will learn one day."

Ruth pulled together ground corn, lard, and goat milk and kneaded the dough on the wood top. "Why have you come? You are not of Moab, are you?"

She shook her head. "My people come from Bethlehem Judah. Famine lays heavy on the other side of Jordan. Elimelech hopes to find better here."

"Is he your family?"

"My husband, yes." Naomi smiled. "And the two boys are our sons, Mahlon and Chillion."

"You have been doubly blessed."

"All children are a blessing. I'm sure your father thinks of you as a blessing."

Ruth paled, shaking her head. "I am wrong. I caused my mother's death, and he will cause mine when the time comes."

"Ruth." An emotion unfamiliar flittered across the strange woman's face. There was noise toward the door, then Naomi would say no more, simply smile.

"Do not burn anything," Father commanded in his deep voice.

Ruth clenched her fingers in remembered pain. "Of course not, Father. You have taught me well."

"Not well enough."

Elimelech joined them. "Thank you for your generosity."

Naomi stirred the bubbling chicken stew, then spoke quiet words to her husband.

After nodding, Elimelech turned to Father. "When we have settled, Naomi prays you will let the girl visit. There is much she can teach her. It is difficult for a girl without a mother. You have been strong to raise her."

Father relaxed his shoulders. "She knows how to work hard. We will see."

Days later, the strangers from the foreign land hadn't been seen. Curiosity burned in Ruth. As soon as she could, she walked away from the house, toward the fields. Beyond sight of the house, she chose to run. With arms spread wide she cut into a field of wheat. The slap of ripening wheat felt like nothing compared to Father's strikes. There were sounds of someone else nearby. For a moment, fear hurt her chest, but the footfalls were too light for Father. She stopped and crouched close to the ground. Steps passed nearby. She let them go a bit further then took off in pursuit. It didn't take long for him to realize someone ran behind him, and he nearly plowed her over when he turned back.

He brushed hair off his face. "I didn't know girls could run."

"I run better than you jump." Ruth lifted her chin.

He laughed. "Saw that, did you? I'm Mahlon."

"I am Ruth." She looked around. "Shouldn't you be helping build your house?"

"We've used all the stone we could find for the foundation. Bricks are cooking. We've got a growing pile of timber to brace the walls." He touched the nearest stalk. "Bethlehem has been dry so long I wanted to remember how growing things feel."

"Is it very different than Moab?"

"Bethlehem's not green like here, but I guess the villages are much the same."

"Why didn't your family want to live in the main town?"

He shrugged. "Being strangers, we accept land where

they offer. What of your family?"

Ruth turned away with a sigh. "Father doesn't always like people nearby."

She studied him in silence. Dark hair, olive tone skin, wide smile, and curious eyes. He seemed to be watching her as well. Ruth rubbed her hands on her dirty dress. "I should go."

"Which way is out?"

Ruth couldn't keep from grinning. "You raced in without knowing the way out?"

"We found our way here, figured I'd be able to get out of a wheat field."

"Ah." She invited him to walk back with her. "Why did you come to Moab?"

He shrugged. "Father came this way as a lad. He remembered it when travelers through Bethlehem spoke of the green girdle beyond the great river."

"Winter comes. It won't be green for long. I hope your house is ready for the change. Here's your path." She showed him the way he should go. Before he could say anything more, she ran.

Bellow of an ox caught her attention as Ruth arrived back at her home. With a handful of hay, she teased the animal, letting it tug bits to eat.

"I thought you went to gather from the field."

Ruth gasped as a hard hand closed around her arm. "I couldn't find mushrooms."

He pushed her away. "That family came by today. The woman asked your help setting up the kitchen. I imagine they have goods stored in their wagon."

She waited to hear more but when he said nothing, she pulled her courage. "Am I to go?"

His lip curled with disdain. "Yes. Will be good to have

a day without you haunting my steps." He stopped at the opening of the stable. Afternoon light left him as a black shadow. A muscle pulsed in his cheek. "I want dinner and then I do not want to see you."

***

Excitement caused Ruth to wake before light broke the veil of night. Stars twinkled in the sky as she wrapped a blanket around her shoulders and looked out from the upper level of the stable. An animal bellowed below and the first of the birds called as the sun peaked over the horizon. If she walked slowly, perhaps it wouldn't be too early by the time she arrived.

She didn't bother with breakfast but nabbed a hard biscuit and half a mug of apple cider. Once away from the house and father's critical eye, Ruth skipped through trees to a path running along a creek. She ate her biscuit, enjoyed the crisp tart flavor of cider, then rinsed her mug in the cool water. The journey continued. She went further than she meant and then doubled back. It was the wild call of the brothers that led her to their burgeoning homestead.

The shorter, lanky brother noticed her first. He was not the one she'd met previously. "What are you doing here?"

Mahlon skid to a stop beside Chillion. "We've met. You live on the farm with the big stable."

"I am Ruth."

He grinned. "I did not forget."

Chillion frowned. "Have you come to spy on us?"

Ruth tilted her head. "I was invited."

Naomi stepped from behind one of the wagons. "She is my guest. Good morning, child. I did not think to see you this early."

"I can come back."

The woman smiled, holding out her hand. "Nonsense. Help me prepare breakfast."

Ruth couldn't stop the smile on her face. For the first time in her young life, she felt welcomed.

***

Less than a month later, Ruth stood beside Naomi looking up at the new house. Though smaller than Father's, the house had a main room with its cooking hearth and shelves for storing supplies. Connecting to that was a room with benches topped with mats for sleeping. Upstairs was another area for when summer heat drove them outside. "You will stay many happy years here."

Naomi watched clouds thicken on the horizon "As long as YHWH provides."

Ruth tilted her head. "Who is YHWH?"

"He is the God of Abraham, Isaac, and Jacob. The one my ancestors followed from Egypt."

Ruth glanced through the courtyard. "I do not see your God."

Naomi laughed. "Because He is not made of wood or stone. We are not to craft graven images of Him."

"Then how do you honor him?"

She sighed. "Each year we would travel to the Tabernacle for the feast days and make our sacrifices as directed by the priests. We are far from the Tabernacle now. Elimelech must pray for YHWH to guide him."

"You could pray to our god if you miss your worship."

"Oh, no, child. YHWH commands we have no other gods before Him."

"He sounds different from anything I have known."

Naomi wrapped an arm across Ruth's shoulder. "I will

teach you of Him. There are stories that help us remember."

Ruth was careful not to move. She could almost imagine having her own mother in the unfamiliar touch.

Chapter Shtaim (two)

Darkening clouds spread and wind picked up. Though Ruth returned home to prepare a meal for Father, her thoughts remained with Naomi's family. Would they know what to do if the storm turned evil? Caught in her concern, the unexpected slap against the back of her head knocked her into the table where she prepared food.

"You think I have time to wait? Where is my meal?"

"I'm sorry." Her heart thudded as she righted a bowl of herbs. "I will set your meal in a moment."

Though the interchange did not take long, Ruth was forced to tend animals as rain began falling. Wind whipped rain through the shelter, and she was soon soaked.

Water helped with the animals. Brushes moved quickly through their pelts. Thick shouldered oxen grunted as they moved closer to the back of the shelter where the stone wall offered a modicum of protection. Ruth felt something in the air as well. Unwilling to be trampled should the animals get frightened, she climbed above them, settling in the corner where she could watch the storm cross the plain.

A finger of cloud reached down from the sky to touch the ground. Wind howled. Rain thickened so the whirling cloud could no longer be seen, but the animals below bellowed. Ruth watched until the sky lightened, and the storm passed. Standing in the opening, her hand clinging to the side of the structure, she peered across the plain. Already, streams of water faded into the earth. Naomi's house was too far away to see. Had they stayed indoors? Ruth hurried down to check the animals, pushing them into the corral to dry as the afternoon cleared. Father didn't stir. Ruth used the path leading around the back and ran to check on her friends.

The storm had not been kind. Though the stone structure remained intact, wind had ripped tents and coverings and pushed debris against the wagons, flipping one of them over. Naomi pulled uselessly on the iron bottom of the wagon. Ruth ran to her side.

"Where are the others?" Ruth heard bleating of sheep.

"He went to bring the animals inside. The storm passed over too quickly."

"Who?"

"Elimelech. I must move this."

"It's too heavy. Let me get Father and other men from the village."

Naomi, her face gray with worry, looked at Ruth and nodded. She closed her eyes and rested her head against a wood plank. Ruth stood uncertainly for a moment before running. Her desire to get help overruled fear of father. She stopped at the door and composed herself.

He noticed when she entered. "What damage have you seen?"

"Nothing of your property, but the strangers need help. The whirling cloud passed through their house."

"A sign they are not wanted here."

"Will you help them? Should I get our neighbors to

help as well?"

Father stood. "He has good knowledge of animals and their care. It will benefit us all to help. You may call our neighbors."

Gathering others didn't take long. Ruth stood beside Naomi as a group of men dug through the debris and shifted the wagon. Mahlon and Chillion joined them. Both young men seemed pale. The Elder of Moab joined their small group with a grave shake of his head. Ruth felt Naomi shake and she grabbed hold of her, fearful the woman was about to fall. But Naomi showed strength. She whispered to her sons, who ran into the house. They returned with a white blanket stitched with flowers and unfamiliar motifs. Ruth remembered seeing it cover the mat where they slept. Naomi bade the boys remain with Ruth.

Mahlon took hold of her hand. A cry rose from Naomi as she disappeared behind the wagon. Ruth felt her chest burn and tears gathered in her eyes. When Naomi returned, her face remained drawn, but no sound shared her anguish.

Men brought the covered body of Elimelech. A hole was dug and before the sun has moved towards its western shore, all had gone, the earth swallowed her corpse, and Naomi sat on the hard ground staring at the place where he had died. She held tight to Ruth's hand without talking for a long while.

Father frowned. "This dead is not yours. Return home."

Ruth slipped her hand from Naomi. "I will come tomorrow."

Father struck Ruth across the face. "What need have they for you?"

Naomi threw her hand out to prevent Mahlon and Chillion getting between Ruth and her father. Ruth covered her cheek, pain waring with embarrassment.

Father smirked at Naomi. "What need have you for a servant?"

Mahlon squared his shoulders. "I am man of the house now. I have learned skill at the side of my father. We will continue to work as he would. More help will be needed at the house.

Father stood still a moment. Ruth waited a few feet distance for his answer. Finally, he nodded. "She will return in the morning."

Ruth did not wait to hear more. She hurried to return home.

***

Naomi tisked as she checked Ruth's cheek, but said nothing. "Orpah?" Ruth noticed another girl from the village hanging in the doorway.

Though younger, Orpah was taller than Ruth. "Mother sent me to help set things in order."

Naomi tilted her lips up in greeting, but the smile did not touch her eyes or heart. "Ruth, prepare a meal while Orpah and I clean the courtyard."

Ruth nodded, though she did not understand the feeling of hurt she felt as Naomi walked away with the other girl.

Kneading bread helped ease her troubled thoughts. Stew simmered. She pulled down bowls then looked at the raised platform on the floor. Elimelech would no longer have his place at the table. Would one of the boys sit there instead? Mahlon was bigger than Chillion. Ruth tore the dough into three parts, rolled each part, then braided the loaf.

***

"What's it like to have a mother?" Ruth asked Mahlon as he walked with her along the trail back home.

"Everyone has a mother."

"I never knew mine. Naomi takes good care of you." He smiled gently. "She would have liked to have a girl. You spend more time with her than either of us."

"Father wanted boys. He does not think I am worth having."

"I do not like his treatment of you." Mahlon's face darkened.

"We do not get to choose who our parents are."

"Thankfully, there are other choices you can make."

Ruth's cheeks warmed at the implication of his words. "Father will make that choice for me. I cannot."

Mahlon put his hands in the pockets of his robes and said no more. Ruth hurried away when they reached her home.

Chapter Shalash (three)

Winter cold gripped the plain and Ruth built up the fire in the kitchen.

"We've got the last of the holes filled in," Chillion said as he wrung water from his hands before holding them closer to the fire.

Ruth paused in sorting dried beans as Orpah colored prettily and drooped her face over her work. Ruth peeked at Chillion. His attention alighted on Oprah for a moment, lingered, then he cleared his throat and left their area.

Ruth stared at Orpah. The bigger girl had become a friend over the past month. "What was that?"

They both resumed their task of sorting debris from the beans.

"What?" Orpah attempted to appear calm.

"Are you interested in the foreigner?"

"Me? What of you? Mahlon follows you everywhere."

She wanted to deny the accusation but couldn't. She dropped her handful of beans into the storage bin. "Wouldn't matter. Father would never consent."

"Consent to what?" Naomi asked as she joined them. Both girls looked down, then at each other and giggled. Naomi didn't need to say anything more, but Ruth like the tiny smile that warded off a layer of sorrow.

Ruth shifted the basket. "One more rinse and these beans should be good for the winter."

"You will have to break ice and be careful not to stay out there too long."

"I will finish this and head home. Now will be the warmest part of the day."

"Remain home as long as the cold lasts. Stay warm."

***

Ruth shivered beneath blankets in the night and thought about Naomi's direction. Father would not permit her to stay near the fire where she could be warm. She'd still go to Naomi. Just a little time near the fire would be worth it. The decision helped her fall into a fitful sleep.

In the morning, the fire didn't seem to give off enough heat to warm her. She prepared Father a small meal, then made the trek to the foreigners while the dew on the dead plants still crackled with ice. Her throat hurt, but that didn't keep her from starting a pan of beans warming with a hock of meat.

"Ruth? What are you doing?" Naomi wrapped a blanket around herself.

"It's warmer here than at home. I thought I would come anyway." Ruth blinked. Naomi looked odd, as though air wavered between them.

Naomi moved to her side and pressed a hand against her forehead. She frowned. "You have a fever."

Ruth shook her head. "I'm too cold for a fever."

"You have one, nonetheless. Come, sit over here." She drew her to a bench.

Ruth sat, but then began to shake. Moments later she was wrapped in blankets, lying down nearer the fire.

Hours later, cold turned hot and she threw the blankets on the floor. Someone moved them out of the way and used a cool rag on her face. Sometime after that, when a cough rattled her breath, Naomi rubbed a concoction on her chest. The smell twisted her head. There was no getting away from it. Her cough eased.

Weak and pale, noticing the length of shadows on the floor, she sat up.

"What are you doing?" Naomi kept her from standing.

"I must return home. Father will be furious."

A soft hand on her shoulder pushed her back on the mat. "Mahlon has gone to speak with your father. You are too sick to return home. You must wait for the sick to pass and the weather to become fair."

"I can't be sick. I have work to do."

Naomi washed Ruth's face. "Cold has caused you harm. I would not lose another person I care about. By YHWH's hand you will remain until you are well."

She must have drifted. Night had fallen. The kitchen fire provided light. Thirst clenched her tongue and throat. She pulled herself up.

"Would be better for you to sleep."

"I'm too thirsty for sleep." She was surprised to find Mahlon by her.

He dipped a cup in a pitcher and handed it to her. "I told Mother to sleep. She is concerned for you."

The cool water refreshed, and she asked for more. Once the thirst had been sated, she stretched back on the mat, curling beneath blankets. Her mind felt clearer than it had all day. "Tell me a story of your people."

"A story?" He was on the floor against a nearby wall. "Mother Rahab was from Jericho, the great walled city of Canaan. She lived in a house on the wall."

Ruth liked the sound of his voice. She closed her eyes and listened, but the sound seemed to float without really saying anything. She slept.

***

Days later, Ruth savored a warmed cup of water with scented leaves. She leaned against the wall facing Naomi. "I'm sorry for the trouble I have caused your family."

"You are not trouble. Our kindness tenfold does not match the kindness you have shown since we arrived in Moab."

"I am grateful you came. It has not been many seasons, but I am happier now than I've ever been."

"One of my sons is especially pleased to know you. Would you mind that he has gone to your father?"

Heat infused her cheeks. Ruth looked down. "Many girls in Moab are married at fourteen."

Naomi smiled. "You are of age, yes. What do you think regarding Mahlon as your husband?"

"Would he not prefer another?"

"He is taken with you." Naomi laughed. "As I believe you are with him."

Ruth clenched her hands. "I would choose him over any other young man I know." Something within herself sparked, and she smiled.

Naomi grinned as well. "Mahlon will speak to your father about marriage."

***

Days later, with her strength returned, Ruth wanted to get home to prepare her things to leave, to take her place with Mahlon. She glanced at him walking beside her. As they lost sight of the house, he stopped and took her hands.

"I know your father's treatment of you may fuel your desire to join me in marriage. I will never treat you as he does. I love you," he said, tucking a strand of hair behind her ear. "I hope you will grow to love me."

"You are dear to me. Your family is dear to me." She tilted her head. "Yet you are different than the others." She squeezed his hands. "I want to be close to you."

He kissed her forehead. "I think we will do well together."

Father stood in the doorway, arms crossed, leaning against the wall as they crossed over the path. His eyes were dark. The flask in his hand spoke to the fact he'd been drinking. Ruth slowed, allowing Mahlon to take the lead.

Father sneered. "I will not take her back. She has chosen her way with strangers."

Mahlon stiffened, but Ruth placed a hand on his shoulder. Standing straight, arms at her side, she moved forward until she stood a few feet away from her father. "You have never wanted me here, but I have cared for the animals. Provided meals for you. I've worked as you have taught. Take an apprentice. Share your knowledge with someone you can respect."

His lip drooped. "Get your things and be gone." He motioned to a pile next to the animal trough.

Ruth hid her shaking as she grabbed a wide, shallow basket. There were other things, but she didn't feel like trying to get past him. After stacking what lay in and around a puddle, she set the basket on her head and turned away. She heard Mahlon's steps behind her. A hint of sadness and what had never been tightened her throat, but something different overpowered it.

Chapter Arba (four)

Time passed. Chillion and Orpah moved to a house in town next to her family. Naomi remained with Mahlon and Ruth. Most mornings, Ruth crossed into the kitchen, greeting her mother-in-law with a kiss as Naomi prepared two mugs with hot tea.

"Good morning, my daughter." Naomi placed the hot cup on the sill of the open window and sat beside Ruth. The chilly breeze was not unpleasantly so, and they watched fog roll across the lane. A slender cat jumped into the window, licked a paw, then jumped toward the sound of a bird in the brush.

Ruth broke the silence first. "Who is the man Chillion spoke of last evening? I never got the chance to ask."

"He is a nobleman or soldier of Israel, if he has come to King Eglon to pay tribute for us."

"He will not mind having a meal with strangers of Moab?"

"He knows you are part of our life here. He did not refuse the offer."

"We should go early. Help Orpah prepare the meal." Ruth grinned. "She is not always gentle with the bread."

Naomi laughed. "You want to meet the man from Israel." She shook her head. "Getting there early will not make him travel any faster."

Ruth shrugged. "We could meet him on the way."

***

They did not. It was hours later, sweet bread cooling by the window, when the guest arrived by horse.

"Master Ehud," Chillion greeted with a bow. "I am pleased you have accepted our invitation to stay." He waved his arm toward the prepared table. "Welcome."

Mahlon stood, and Ruth jumped up beside him. The man was younger than she expected.

The guest bowed toward the family. "I did not expect such hospitality in Moab."

Naomi joined them. "The drought crippled our home in Bethlehem. Elimelech received an offer to come to Ka-Tamir. Though he did not feel as though he could refuse, I believe our time here has been blessed." She smiled at Ruth and Orpah.

Ehud stood until Naomi sank into her seat at the head of the table. Chillion indicated he should take the seat to her right. Ehud stepped aside and allowed his servant to reset the silverware at his space.

Naomi frowned. "Are you well?"

"My apologies," Ehud smiled to show no insult. "My family has a rare trait. My hand of strength is to my left, not to the right, as all of you."

Ruth tried not to stare as the meal progressed, but it was unusual to see the natural workings of her hand reflected opposite in the guest across the table from her. "Are you also of Bethlehem?"

He shook his head. "No, I am of the tribe of Benjamin. Much of my life has been lived in Gilead. It is only recently I have traveled through the lands of Israel."

"Is that how you came to offer tribute to King Eglon?" Mahlon narrowed his eyes.

His lips twitched. "I have a present for him from the tribes. Call it tribute if you wish." He turned to Naomi. "Did your husband expect to return to Bethlehem?"

"I suspect when the drought ceased. I have heard no such news."

He smiled. "Consider yourself assured. The rains have come. We are in a second season. YHWH has remembered us."

"Blessed be his name." She glanced at her sons. "I am not sure what there would be to return to. Many years have passed."

Chillion raised his glass. "In the spring, my brother and I could go for you. Set your house to rights and then bring you back to Bethlehem."

Ehud nodded. "It would be well for you to return to your country. It is where you belong, not in these foreign lands."

Naomi's eyes glistened. "I am ready to go home."

Though the meal finished, and daylight dwindled, the company remained at the table. Ehud tapped his hand and looked at the brothers. "The day will soon come when you will be asked to defend Israel from these strangers of Moab. Are you prepared to battle?"

Mahlon cleared his throat as he glanced at his younger brother. "We will assist as we may, but you forget. We have lived among Ka-Tamir most our lives. To you, they are strangers, but to us, they are neighbors. These small villages are as oppressed by the hand of the King as any in Israel."

He shook his head. "It is a pity your father did not survive to teach you the ways of our people. I have been called here for a purpose. That purpose will be fulfilled."

Naomi lifted her glass, demonstrating her right as

elder to be heard. "The open is not the place to speak of intent. There is a quiet room upstairs that can be used for such purpose."

"You speak well. Thank you, my lady," Ehud said, then looked at the brothers for direction. The three men left the table.

Ruth helped Orpah carry remains of the meal to the washing area. Orpah scraped debris into a pail as Ruth poured water into a bucket. Orpah frowned. "Our life here is not so bad. Why should they want to take us away from Ka-Tamir?"

"Mother Naomi longs for home. I would make the journey so her joy may be complete."

Orpah sighed. "From the stories she tells of shops on the hills, I wonder if we could find that soft fabric made by travels coming from the far east."

Mahlon waved to Ruth from the bottom step. "I will remain to speak with the men. You should return home with Naomi."

"Go now," Orpah pushed her toward the front of the house. "There is still a little light, but you can take a lantern from the front. We'll bring it back tomorrow."

Ruth held the light with one hand and linked arms with Naomi with the other. Twinkling stars gleamed overhead. "Master Ehud seems different than other men of Israel who have visited."

"The hand of YHWH is with him."

"Have you met him before?"

She shook her head. "I have been to the City of the Tabernacle, but never traveled elsewhere until we came here. My family had been forty years in the Promise Land when I was born. Father never wanted to go further than necessary." She grinned. "I must be like him. Leave me with my family and I am content."

"I would like to see your country one day. Would that be possible?"

"YHWH's plans are greater than mine. "

Sounds of the village faded as they walked the path toward home. Stars shone against the black sky overhead as they reached the house.

Chapter Hamesh (five)

By morning, Mahlon had not yet come home. "Orpah may need help cleaning up, I'll return to the village." Ruth stopped Naomi from pouring a second cup of tea.

Naomi started to stand, but Ruth placed a hand on her shoulder. "Stay here. I'm sure your knees can use a rest after walking there and back yesterday."

"Tell Orpah to send for me if I am needed." She waved as Ruth left through the open doorway into the garden. She grabbed the cooled lantern to take with her.

There were others in the house, but Ruth didn't see Mahlon or Chillion. Some of the voices were angry, though she could not hear what was said. She pushed through a group lurking by the front door. She recognized Orpah's dark hair and headed in her direction.

"Are you well?" Ruth asked as she set the lantern on the table.

Orpah sat with her brother, Dervah. "A terrible thing has happened." Orpah gripped Dervah's hand. "Tell her."

He motioned for Ruth to sit across from them. "King Eglon is dead. That Israelite dog killed him."

Ruth stared at Orpah. "You don't mean…"

She nodded. "We had the evening meal with him last night."

"But how? Ehud is a slender man. How could he kill someone as large as King Eglon?"

"By devilish craft, it can't be natural." Dervah glared out the window. "He wore a sword that could be drawn with his left hand. None of the guards thought to look for such a thing. He made such a pretty presentation of the gift." Dervah waved his arm. "I was invited. We were leaving when the dog said he had a special message for the king. He was alone with him in the spring house. Stabbed our king and left him for dead."

"What happens now?" Orpah squeezed his hand.

"There will be war, although how we're to manage without a leader…" He peered at Ruth. "Your husband will fight for Moab?"

She frowned. "You can't ask him to do that. The Israelites are his people. They're our people now." She glanced at Orpah.

"If there is to be any fighting, it will be to get Moab out of their land. We should not be needed. There's enough work to do tilling the land for planting. We have no time to fight." Orpah released Dervah.

"For your sake, I hope it does not come this far." Dervah stood. His sister tugged at her lower lip with her teeth but said nothing more. With a grunt, he took his leave. The others followed.

Ruth watched him leave. "What does this mean?"

Orpah shrugged. "They've been captives of Moab since before I was born."

"I hope they gain their freedom before a successor to the king is chosen. Should we tell the others?"

"I wonder if Ehud explained his plan to Mahlon and

Chillion last night. They talked until early hours of the morning."

"Where are they?" Ruth glanced at the stairs, expecting to see her husband lurking in the shadows.

"Jayin found dead cattle in his field. He asked for their help."

Ruth cringed. "I hope they swim in the river before they come home. I don't want the scent of dead cow lingering in my house."

They continued cleaning up the house, lamenting the struggles of husbands who worked with animals.

Ruth returned home early in the afternoon. A cool wind blew from the north. Puffs would stir up bits of dirt and dust. A cardinal sang high in a tree. Peace surrounded her, and she skipped along the path. What harm could come from so beautiful a day?

Chapter Shesh (six)

Harm hadn't come that day. Months later, long after word of war had come and gone, and Israel no longer paid tribute to Moab, sickness invaded the land. Ruth stared at the mound in the ground. Mahlon lay beside his brother, Chillion, who's grave in the earth was two days older.

Orpah's voice rose in lament. Other criers joined her, a mourning dirge across Moab. Ruth remained silent, tears testament to the well of hurt within. Ten years of happiness felled by disease. These two weren't the only ones, merely the latest. Ruth sighed, then sat at the foot of her husband. She lowered her head against the mound of dirt. A smear across her forehead marked her breaking heart. She remained prostrate until someone pulled her in as night fell.

Morning light did not alleviate the wounds of death. Silence hovered in the house. Ruth crossed over to the kitchen then started at the sight of Naomi sitting on a bench with the cat in her lap.

She was pale and drawn. Gray had suddenly sprung into her hair. She didn't cry, just sat, a stoic statue of death's doom. Ruth shivered, and she ran to Naomi's side and held her hands. Amure, the cat, leapt away. Naomi kissed the side of her head. "I spoke with Mahlon at the start of this week. War has ended. Israel is free. I thought we could return home." She glanced at Ruth with teary eyes. "You would like Bethlehem. In the spring when rain comes as it should, tiny yellow flowers burst through the fields. They make a beautiful sight." Her chest shuddered as she drew a breath. "Now I have no sons, and no husband." Her words seemed lost, as did the despair in her eyes.

Ruth wrapped her arms around Naomi. Though neither of them cried, their hurt could not be eased. Ruth finally straightened. "Now is not forever. Perhaps you will find hope in Bethlehem."

"I think it is the right thing. We will fit what we can in the wagon and take the road over to Israel, then onto Bethlehem."

Ruth didn't mind having something to do, anything to do to keep her mind from the mound of dirt. Mahlon's crooked grin toyed with her thoughts as she wrapped a comb in his shirt and shoved it in the bottom of the bag that would carry her things. Her pack remained light, but not so her heart. She moved to the kitchen.

She fit what she could in the crate that would go in the wagon. Not everything, but surely it would be enough for the three of them to start anew.

Ruth wiped sweat from her face. What would Bethlehem be like? What would they think of her, a Moabite?

***

Another day dawned. Ruth grunted as she tugged on the lead for the oxen. The burly pair moved with a low bellow. "Mahlon never had this much trouble with you," she muttered as she twisted to get the harness to hook onto the wagon.

Orpah blinked as she dropped a basket with blankets in the wagon. "Tati Orthina knit the receiving blanket. I always thought Chillion and I would have a son." Her chin quivered as she took a deep breath.

Ruth brushed hair from her eyes as she joined Orpah. "You may find another husband."

"Among the foreigners?" Orpah said with a quiet voice.

"You loved one of them well enough. Why not another?"

Orpah sighed but said nothing more as Naomi joined them. The older woman wore a black shawl over her gray gown. The dull colors made her face seem bleaker and eyes dull. Ruth ran to her side. "We have packed all that will fit. I fear anymore and we'll leave a trail of belongs on the road." The cat jumped up on the side of the wagon. "I suppose there is room for Amure."

Naomi's lips softened. "You have done well." She glanced at Orpah. "Both of you have, though you mourn as I do."

Ruth squeezed Naomi's hand. "We are ready to leave."

They both looked at the house. Ruth felt fresh tears burn her throat. Waving at Mahlon as he came home from the fields. Swatting at him because of the dirt trailing across the floor.

Naomi drooped. "There is no reason to stay."

A sob escaped from Orpah. The three women wrapped arms round each other. Ruth finally pulled away. "If we are to go, then we should go now." Ruth pulled herself onto the ledge in the front of the wagon, then leaned over to give Naomi a hand.

***

With Orpah's help from behind, Naomi managed to make her seat in the front of the wagon. Ruth sat on her left holding the leads for the oxen with the switch at her feet. Orpah sat on the right. Not even the flowers sprinkled across the front of the house broke through the gray that marred her vision. Both boys gone. What if they had fought? What if she'd pushed them to follow Master Ehud and fight against the Moabites? But neither wanted to and she hadn't pushed. She didn't dare look at Ruth and Orpah. Did they blame her for the deaths of their husbands? Orpah's words clung like bitters to her heart. The children of Israel were foreigners to them. What hope was there for them? Childless and destitute in Bethlehem?

Ruth shifted as she urged the oxen to turn onto the road to the north. Naomi laid her hand on Ruth's leg. "Wait. Let us down here."

Ruth gave her a look, but she pulled to stop the animals. The creak of wooden wheels quieted, and the rocking back and forth stilled.

Orpah wiped tears from her face as she searched across the fields. "You want to stand here?"

"Yes, please."

There was nothing significant about the fields, save for the paths leading through them to the village. Naomi hardened herself against the unbearable parting that remained. As the three of them stood, she grasped both their hands. "Go. Return each of you to your mother's house. May the Lord deal kindly with you, as you have dealt with the dead and with me." Naomi felt Ruth's hand tighten, and she leaned her head against Ruth's shoulder. "The Lord grant you may find rest, each of you in a house with a new husband."

Orpah sobbed. "But we mean to go with you."

"You cannot ask us to watch you leave alone."

Though her heart broke, she pulled away from the young women. "Turn back, my daughters. Do I have sons yet to bear that they may become your husbands? Turn back and go your way for I am too old to find another husband. Even if I did, and bear a son next year, would you wait until he was such an age? Would you refrain from marrying another while you were yet in your youth?" Her voice broke and the three of them stood crying. "No, my daughters. It is bitter to me for your sakes that the hand of the Lord has turned against me. Go home, and may you not know further pain."

Orpah threw her arms around Naomi. "How am I to bear parting? But my brother was wounded in battle and I may yet be able to help his family."

Naomi kissed her forehead. "Go in peace. May the Lord bring you blessing that he has taken through me."

Orpah then hugged Ruth. "Will you return with me?"

"I cannot, my home is not that direction."

Orpah grabbed a bag from the wagon and reached for the blanket. Her hand shook and she didn't touch it. "I can't." Sobbing, she held her things close to her chest. Her red-rimmed eyes looked once more on Naomi, and then she ran, turning her back on them.

Ruth sobbed as she sucked in air. Naomi turned to her. With weary age she had not felt until today, she wrapped an arm around the young woman and drew her close. "Your sister-in-law has gone back to her people. She has returned to her gods. It is time now for you to go."

But Ruth shook her head, staring up at Naomi. "I cannot. You must not ask it of me. If I don't go with you now, I will follow after. Where you go, I will go. Where you live, I will live there with you. Your people will be my people, and your God will be my God. I will be with you until death, and where you are laid, there will I lay also. May the Lord do evil to me and more also if anything, but death separates me from you."

Naomi felt her legs weaken and they both slid to the ground, unwilling to part. Ruth finally leaned back, wiping her cheeks as they both chuckled. Naomi shook her head. "My darling daughter, this is a long road. I have no assurance YHWH will protect us. What do I do if something happens to you?"

Ruth grasped both her hands. "We have each other. We have a strong pair of cattle to help carry the load."

"With barely enough to feed them, let alone ourselves."

Ruth brushed back her hair. She stood, shaking her skirt of dust and debris before stretching a hand to aid Naomi. "I am with you no matter what. Let us greet the fate laid on our path."

It still hurt, climbing back in the wagon. Her aching bones protested the rumbling rock of the wagon. Her heart grew bleak at the look across the plain of Moab. Too much of her heart remained buried in the ground, eaten by death. But Ruth, sitting straight as she looped the leads for the oxen over a rail, gave her courage to continue.

Book 2: The Story of Boaz and Ruth
Third Week of the Month of Nisan
Chapter Sheva (seven)

"Here's a tree for shade. We should rest a moment," Ruth guided Naomi toward a copse and helped her sit with her back against a trunk of the tree. She offered her water from the pouch.

"Thank you, my daughter," Naomi drank.

Ruth sat beside her, listening. "What strange insects are those in the fields?"

"Crickets, no doubt." She glanced across the fields rolling from the road to meet the mountain on the horizon. "Must be about time for barley harvest, those crops look ready to burst."

"Are we close to your home?"

"My home?" She sighed. "Not sure I have one. Elimelech's father settled part of Bethlehem. We had a house, of course. Some land. Turned to dust in the drought." Her eyes remained dull. "How can I know what remains?"

Ruth took her hand. "A roof over our heads will be a start." She stared at the yellow grasses waving in a gentle spring wind. "Could we get permission to go into the field and gather grain enough to live?"

"Of course." She leaned her head against the tree.

"How could I have forgotten? There is no need to ask. Once the harvesting begins, we can gather after the reapers. It is a provision of God for the poor and the needy." Naomi clutched her shawl. "Have I become such as they?" She closed her eyes.

Ruth grasped hold of her hands. "You have endured much, especially these last two weeks following the King's Highway, crossing the great river, and now finally turning south again towards Bethlehem. Your God provided our way."

Naomi touched Ruth's face, her eyes gleaming with unshed tears. "Dear daughter, He is your God as well. You keep me from despair."

Ruth smiled. "Are you ready? The animals look rested." She clucked for the pair of oxen grazing nearby. They met her at the wagon pole. In a moment, she had their harnesses attached. A strange sound drew her attention as she pulled the lead to get the cart back on the road. The oxen plowed on. Ruth went to the wagon and pulled a corner aside. "What have we here?" Amure the cat had three little kittens kneading their tiny paws against her stomach.

"Is something wrong?" Naomi moved closer.

Ruth grinned at her. "We've had some kittens added to the wagon."

"Amure?"

"Good thing I didn't leave her behind. If we mean to live in a house that's been empty fifteen years, we may want a mouser. Or two." She returned the cover to its place and took hold of the lead for the animals.

Naomi kept pace beside her. "We'll start seeing stone walls which mark territories of the fields." Her eyes took on a dreamy glaze. "When I was young, I would have known which belonged to whom. I could have told which fields to keep away from because their workers are evil."

"Evil?" Ruth shivered. "Would they harm us?"

"Some may take advantage if they can. Probably no one remembers us."

"The one you saw in Moab. He told you the drought was over. Didn't he know you?"

Naomi sighed. "We've enough sorrows to burden our day. I shouldn't be thinking about more."

They walked in companionable silence until a little peach-colored bird raced across the road in front of them. "Was that a bird?" Ruth tried to push up to see over the oxen, but she could not.

Naomi smiled. "Another sign we are close to home."
***
The road took a familiar turn, and Naomi burst into tears. Thick walls following the hills hadn't been built by the children of Israel. Neither had the shops, houses, avenues—what she knew from childhood had been built by Canaanites, now long departed. Elimelech's family took property in the northeast not far from the fields. They didn't need to go through the gates. Naomi took a shuddering breath as she pointed to a trail that wrapped along the walls. "Go this way. Hold the animals on the inside as we climb." The way seemed better than she remembered. There were new houses, a break in the wall she didn't remember, and a view of crops.

Ruth gasped. "The fields seem to go forever."

"There is plenty of work to be done. The softer-looking plants are the barley. You can see workers there already. Wheat is still weeks from being ready." Trees and brush cut through the scene. Short walls as well. "Elimelech has a small field there somewhere." She chuckled without mirth. "Probably where the brambles and brush are thickest."

Ruth led the oxen onto a road. "Is your house on this main avenue?"

Naomi shook her head. "We'll turn up there. Not much else, at least there wasn't when we lived here years ago." She held her breath as Ruth followed directions. Memories jumbled with the present. What if someone had taken the house? Or had it crumbled and fallen away?

What came into view wasn't either thought. The property was overgrown, although someone must have done a little work to keep it manageable. A torn curtain fluttered through a window. What remained of the thatched roof would not do much against the season of storms. Or the cold.

Ruth wrapped her arm around Naomi. "It's a lovely place."

Naomi really did chuckle. "Are we looking at the same place?"

Ruth led the animals across a rut and into what would be the courtyard.

"Away with you, we'll allow no squatters here." A young man brandishing a long stick yelled as he neared.

The oxen grunted, pawing nervously. Ruth gripped the lead. "Are you mad? These animals are not safe to startle."

"You shouldn't have them here in the first place," he argued, but lowered the stick and slowed to a walk. "This is family property, and you aren't family."

Naomi removed her travel scarf. "I am family. This is Elimelech's house, and I am Elimelech's wife."

The young man crossed his arms and frowned. "You

don't look like nobody I know."

She shook her head. "I've been gone fifteen years. You were a lad. Why would you recognize me now? Where is your mother? Your aunts or grandmother?"

An older woman turned the corner and joined them. "Naomi? Is that you?"

Bitterness swelled through her. "Do not call me Naomi. I have lost the blessing of the Lord. He has turned life to sorrow. Call me Mara." She moved stiffly to the rock circling the well and sat. "I went away full, and the Lord has brought me back empty. Why call me Naomi when the Lord has testified against me and the Almighty has brought calamity upon me?"

"Oh, daughter," she grasped Naomi's hands. "You have life. The Lord may yet bring you blessing."

***

Ruth blinked as her eyes moistened, seeing Naomi's pain, and feeling the ache of her own loss. "Is this the house where we will live?" The open courtyard was surrounded on three sides by a stone building. Several doorways led into different areas of the house and stairs led up to a porch and another room.

The man looked at the other woman. She nodded. "Yes, this is Naomi's house." She changed her words at the sight of Naomi's pain. "Mara. Let me call others. We will need to set the corners."

Ruth frowned as she glanced through an open door. "Set what corners?"

The older woman chuckled. "We need to clean the house and make it livable."

Ruth lowered her head, heat filling her cheeks, but others arrived and took attention from her.

"Naomi!" More women declared as they came upon

her in the house.

Ruth used a rag to wipe spider webs from the window opening. The women wore long gowns with an overtunic tied around the waist. Their earth tone colors were muted compared to the green skirt Ruth wore. Once the few windows were cleaned, Ruth went to the wagon to retrieve ceramic jars and clay bins to put in the cooking area. An older woman with a turban-like wrap around her head swept the hard floor and watched Ruth. Ruth placed the jugs she carried in a corner.

The older woman clicked as Naomi came in. "You bring a foreign woman with you?"

Naomi smiled at Ruth. "She is my daughter, the only good to have come with me from Moab."

"It is not wise to bring foreigners among us. Ehud delivered us from the Moabite king and his control over us."

"I have seen that king. Even in Kir-Moab the royal court required tribute of us."

Ruth moved beside Naomi. "Mahlon and Chillion worked hard to provide what we needed."

Naomi sighed. "Now we have no one and nothing."

"I will go to the fields. If we save enough seed, next year we'll plant our own crop."

"The sun has already moved toward the west. The house will not ready itself." The older woman took her broom to another area.

Another woman laughed. She wore no covering on her head. Her skin seemed paler than the others. "The women of Israel do not easily trust strangers. Give it time, she will come to know you."

"Are you a stranger?" Ruth asked.

"I am Rahab's daughter, Serena. My mother was of

the great city of Jericho, destroyed by God."

"An entire city destroyed?"

Naomi clapped her hands. "There will be time for stories around the fires of evening. Men laid mounds of hay for sleeping. You may set our bed rolls on them."

Ruth looked across the courtyard. "Where will we sleep?"

"Up on the balcony. We can catch what breezes move in the dark. Use the heavier blankets. Will be cool now, but come high summer…" She didn't need to describe the long hot nights.

Ruth moved their sleeping supplies to the upper area, then set up the water trough on the cobblestone paved area where the animals would be kept. Amure and her litter were given a small blanket in the corner of the kitchen. From the top of the stairs, she could see other houses built much the same way, although they weren't as close as those in the heart of Bethlehem.

After carrying bags of clothing to the second-floor room, Ruth followed the stairs to the roof. The sun was partially obstructed by clouds. They would need to light fires soon before night fell. To the east were fields, and somewhere beyond them the sea. To the west, behind the city, rose mountains separating them from an even greater sea. Naomi joined her, wrapping an arm around her shoulder. Ruth rested her head against Naomi.

"I feel as though I have never left, and yet so much is different."

"You have a good family. Serena and Oma have brought dinner for us. Will they stay and tell stories?"

Naomi smiled. "There will be many nights of stories. They want to know of life in Moab. Many of them knew my sons."

"I want to hear about Mother Rahab."

"I knew her well. Elimelech was her cousin. She passed while we were gone. I fear many did."

They stood a few minutes longer, listening as stonechats sang in a nearby field. Other passerines called as they hunted insects drawn out by the setting sun. By the time they returned to the cooking porch on the other side of the kitchen area, Naomi and Ruth joined a small group of women and children meandered through the house.

Chapter Shmone (eight)

Early the next morning, Ruth pulled the strap of a large pouch over her head, so it crossed her body.

"These may help," Naomi said as she offered a pair of leather gloves, one finger missing. "Mahlon used them as a boy. They should be small enough for you."

Ruth rubbed her fingers across the broken leather. "He must have got into some mischief."

"Take this as well," Naomi held up a belt with a dagger. "Wear it beneath your waist wrap. If there is trouble."

Ruth removed her faded yellow waist wrap and allowed Naomi to tighten the strap of the belt comfortably. The dagger in its scabbard set near her right hand where she could grab it easily. "You think I will have trouble?"

"Not everyone is kind to the poor. You are young. Pretty. They should know you are not without protection."

"I will search for a safer field."

"YHWH watch over you and direct your steps," Naomi offered a blessing as she helped Ruth put the waist wrap in place again.

Early morning sun surrounded Ruth as she walked from Naomi's house to the road leading down into fields.

Rock walls marked boundaries of fields. Great stone buildings could be seen on the far side. Reapers were already at work. She watched a tall, dark man sweep a scythe through the grains. Large bundles stood in piles. There were others as well. Naomi crossed into a nearby field through the opening in the stone wall. She slid among the small group of women and children on their knees, pulling at the plants in the corner. Mahlon's gloves did not fit well, but they helped her grip and pull plants from the earth.

The woman beside her had a baby on her back. His arms waved as he gurgled. His dark eyes sparkled as Ruth made a face. The woman smiled.

"His name is Elway. I am Maria."

"My name is Ruth." She handed her a portion of what she'd pulled.

Maria hesitated, then added it to her bag. "I have not seen you before."

"I am a stranger, although my mother-in-law is known. Naomi. Do you know of her?"

"Of course. My mother, Hananiah, was a servant in her house. I heard she had returned, though not as well as she went away."

They moved on. "Mahlon, her son, was my husband. Last year, great disease came after the war. Mahlon did not fight against his brothers in the war, but he could not stave off disease. He and his brother died."

"What of Elimelech?"

"More than ten years since he died by a horrid storm. Naomi has suffered greatly. I pray she will find peace once more among her kindred." She gave Maria more of what she gleaned. The boy reached for a strand of barley.

"My husband died in war. I did not expect a son. He

has brought joy."

"I can imagine. We had no children. Naomi thinks I should find a new husband."

"It is a tradition that a family member redeems one who has died and brings up seed in his name."

"I am a foreign woman. I doubt a son of Israel will want to marry me." She signed. "I am content to remain with Naomi. I will care for her as any daughter cares for her mother."

"Mistress Maria," a man drenched in sweat and dirt held a flagon of water. The women stopped and pulled cups from their bags. He filled the cups and then sprinkled a few drops on the boy's face. Elway giggled.

He nodded at Ruth. "We have not met."

"I am Naomi's daughter-in-law, Ruth."

He smiled. "I heard she returned. Is it true her husband and both sons died? I knew the boys when I was young."

"It is a difficult time for her."

"And you," Maria spoke up. "You were married to Mahlon."

Ruth blushed. "I could not bear the thought of leaving Naomi. I forced her to bring me."

Maria grasped her hand. "I am certain you have been a help for her."

The man stood, and his soft smile for Maria made Ruth think he cared for the widow. He cleared his throat. "I need to move on. Be well."

"We will." Maria answered, her eyes following him.

Ruth adjusted the strap of her pouch. Maria possibly cared as well. "Our bags won't fill themselves. We should return to work."

Though the day warmed, and Ruth had to use her head scarf to wipe sweat from her eyes, she and Maria continued to pull from the corner. A man stepped toward Ruth, but Maria stood, hands on her hips, glaring. He wiped his forehead and returned to the harvest.

"What was that?" Ruth wondered.

Maria adjusted Elway who slept. Ruth helped her fix the carrier, so his head rested comfortably.

Maria shook her head. "He's a sly one. Tries to force himself. He'd be a danger if I wasn't under the protection of the master of the field."

"Who is the master?"

***

"Master Boaz," Daniel greeted as the older man slid from his horse. He grabbed the rein to keep the animal steady.

Boaz adjusted his cloak and smoothed the blue fringe on the sleeves. "How are the harvesters?"

Daniel walked with Boaz across the terrace of the barn to the edge of the field. "Gimble has returned from last harvest. He moves them quickly. Severn and Aish will harness the mules to gather the sheaves in an hour."

Boaz watched his servants. As he gazed toward the gleaning corners, an unfamiliar woman stood. From the distance, he could tell little about her, and yet, his gaze remained on her. She helped Maria by adding to her bag. "Who is that woman?"

Daniel peered in the same direction. "Maria?"

Boaz ignored Daniel's reddening ears. "No, the woman with her."

"Ah. I spoke with her earlier. Her name is Ruth. Naomi's daughter-in-law."

"Naomi?" Why was the name familiar? "My cousin Elimelech's wife?"

"The same."

"The Lord has finally brought them back. I remember him well."

"Only Naomi and Ruth, sir. Elimelech and his two sons died in the land of Moab."

"Call the reapers. I have a drink for them." He pulled two flagons of robust wine from the bags on the horse. Each man received a measure of two fingers. He lifted his own cup to them. "The Lord be with you," he toasted.

They held their cups in response. "The Lord bless you." The drink served its purpose, refreshing them for an afternoon of toil.

Daniel was about to return the flagon to the bag when Boaz stopped him. "Call the gleaners. The day is warm. They can use refreshing as well."

A dozen women, two holding hands with young children and Maria with Elway on her back, gathered around Boaz and Daniel, along with a few men. Rueben, though almost as old as Boaz, had the innocent gaze of a child. Boaz smiled at him. "Are you well, this season?"

Reuben nodded. "Right as gold." Daniel handed him a cup with a finger of wine.

"The Lord be with you," Boaz offered the same blessing as he had to the reapers.

"The Lord bless you," many of them replied.

He greeted each of the ones he knew by name, even taking time to let Elway tug on his finger. "He's a fine lad, Maria. Bonem is honored." He turned to Ruth, and Boaz felt compassion for the female stranger. "I hear you have been caring for Naomi?" At Ruth's nod, he continued. "I was shocked to hear Elimelech and both sons died in Moab. I teased them horribly when they were young."

"It did no harm to their development. They were both

good men. Hard workers."

"Whom did you marry?"

"Mahlon."

"Ah, yes, I remember their names now. Mahlon and Chillion. Did they ever learn to climb trees without breaking an arm?"

"Not many trees to climb across the plain. Olive trees do not work too well. Chillion did manage to fall from a horse and break his arm. Orpah scolded him for playing around."

"His wife? Did she return with you as well?"

She shook her head. "She returned to her family, with Naomi's blessing. I could not bear the thought of leaving Naomi. I would have followed her if she hadn't acquiesced."

"Many are grateful you did."

"I should return to gleaning."

"Of course, but you must promise to stay in my fields. Work with Maria and the other women. You will be safe."

"Thank you, my Lord."

Boaz watched her return to Maria. After checking the other fields, he had no reason to remain.

"Would you like your horse saddled?" Daniel swatted a fly pestering the stallion.

"I think I would rather join the reapers for today's meal. Invite the gleaners as well."

"We don't usually do that."

"It is well for today. We have plenty of food and wine."

Daniel bowed. "As you wish, sir."

Chapter Tesha (nine)

"I did not think to bring fruit or anything to eat." Ruth stretched, then noticed Maria struggling to unwind the baby carrier. "Here, let me help." She took Elway from the carrier, bouncing him gently on her hip as Maria removed the wrap.

"I'll share what I have. Let me change Elway."

The young overseer returned. "Mistress Maria, Sir Boaz has requested the gleaners join us for the meal."

"Us? We've never been invited before."

"It is wonderous." Daniel agreed. "Allow me to carry this for you." He gathered the carrier and Maria's grain bag.

"My thanks," Maria said, then took Elway from Ruth.

Ruth grinned, following a few steps behind.

***

"Lord Boaz," Ruth was surprised to see him standing at the edge of the tent erected for the meal. Unlike the young reapers and overseers, Boaz' dark hair was sprinkled with silver. His face, although unlined, had the look of age. He had discarded the silken outercoat, but his shoulders remained wide and thick. Ruth felt heat in her cheeks. Surely, a touch of sun. She had no purpose noticing the thickness of his shoulders.

"My daughter," he touched his forehead and bowed in greeting. "Would you honor me by taking lunch at my table? I desire to hear more of my family in Moab."

"I am the one honored, sir. Are you sure?"

"Please," he said as he motioned to a table where Daniel poured olive oil into a shallow bowl.

Ruth tilted her head. "May Maria join us?"

Maria started to protest, but at Boaz' nod, Ruth drew her over. Maria frowned at Ruth and missed the pleased gleam of Daniel.

The young man reached for Elway. "There is a place you can lay a blanket for the child over here."

At Boaz' raised brow, Ruth grinned and sat on a cushion at the table.

"You have worked hard." He broke a bit of bread from the loaf and handed it to her. "Please, there is wine and oil for dipping."

Ruth thanked him again. The tang of wine was smoothed by olive oil.

"Here, my servants have prepared grain cakes. The darker cakes are sweetened with honey. The others have herbs. Take what you would like then share the platter with the others."

Ruth took a sweet and herbed. Boaz offered more bread. A servant brought a drinking bowl with water.

Ruth sighed deeply as the sweet water quenched her thirst. "Thank you again for the honor. You said you desire to learn of our time in Moab?"

"When did you first meet?"

"They took a house at the edge of the village. The king gave him the land. Father was the nearest neighbor. Most of the village resented land given to a son of Israel. He turned out having a talent for animals. By the time he died, all resentment had been forgotten."

"How did he die?"

"A terrible storm brought wind that swirled like a funnel. Mahlon and Chillion proved they could work as well."

"Marrying you must have helped."

"I am no one of consequence." Ruth looked down.

"It was not an arranged marriage?"

"No."

"You must have loved him greatly."

"He was a good man. Thank you for allowing this time of rest. I feel we should return to the gleaning."

"Remember to stay with Maria and the other women. You will be safe."

Ruth bowed her head. "Your kindness is overwhelming. I do not deserve it."

"The comfort and aid you bring Naomi warrant you honor. Go with God's grace."

Ruth helped Maria tuck Elway in his harness. Their bags were not yet half full.

***

Boaz leaned back and watched the women cross the field. They were laughing, though he could not hear them. Ruth waved her arms to amuse the baby. Daniel moved to scold a reaper for a crude remark, but Boaz halted him. "A moment. Instruct your reapers they are to allow Ruth to glean among the sheaves. She is to walk after them as they pick up the sheaves. Have them pull some out from the bundles."

"Sir, that is unheard of." Daniel protested.

"Rebuke her not. Her mother-in-law is kin. She has returned empty and destitute. I will not have it so."

"Of course not, forgive me. She may need help

beating out the barley."

"Help her as you may. The woman with the baby as well." Boaz handed Daniel a satchel with leftover bread and grain cakes. "Give this to Ruth. I will have wine and oil delivered."

"Very good, sir." Daniel knotted the top of the satchel to make it easier to carry.

Boaz stood. "Instruct the reapers there is to be none of the crassness we just witnessed. They are to respect the women, and not touch them. Anyone who does will be released from service without compensation."

"Of course, sir. I will remind them."

***

Ruth looked at Maria when a reaper waved for them. She kept her hand near the knife as they approached the dark man with heavy creases across his forehead.

He bowed to them. "My Lord Boaz invites you to glean among the sheaves. You may follow the cart and take what is left as they collect the bundles. Follow the cart to the barn and we will help you cull the grains to take home with you."

Maria stared at him. "Why would such liberty be afforded us?"

He shrugged. "I can't say, Miss. I wasn't told that. Just that you are permitted to follow the cart and take what is left."

Maria looked at Ruth with brightened eyes. "This must be your doing."

"I can't imagine why. We should hurry, the cart's already at the hill."

The cart moved faster than they could pick up. Handfuls seemed to be scattered for them. Though they still bent to pick up, without having to tear the plants from the earth, they moved quickly, and their pouches filled.

Ruth packed a handful. "I'll start losing parts myself, if the bottom doesn't burst and dump it all."

Maria giggled. "We'll have enough to sell. Will this only be today? Imagine if we get this full every day for the next seven weeks!"

"The barley and the wheat? We could sell at the Farmers Markets through summer. Save enough to plant in the field behind the house."

"Ladies, let us help you with those burdens." Daniel and Reuben joined them near the barn.

Maria smiled. "Good thing Elway is small as he is."

"We will help you cull the grains. We will save the thick straw and bake bricks for you. Your houses will need repairs before next winter. Would you like the fine straw? Do you keep any animals?"

Ruth nodded. "We have a pair of oxen. And cats, but they're likely to play in it."

"I have a goat and a donkey," Maria lowered her head.

"Then we will send the fodder with you as well. In a separate bag. Bring your donkey on the morrow and he'll make easy work of carrying it home for you. He can stay in the barn."

Ruth watched the process of separating the stalks from the actual grains. It was quickly achieved with help from the men. The pouch returned filled with grain.

***

"A long day for you, daughter." Naomi greeted Ruth at the door. "But what is this?" She wondered as she took the pouch filled with grain and a bag of feed.

"I also received this gift," Ruth smiled as she handed Naomi the bag of bread and cakes.

"Where did you glean? Who has shown such kindness?"

Ruth helped carry the supplies to the kitchen area. "Where should we store the grain? It will need to dry before it gets put away."

"There are bins on the porch. It is so much! Blessed be the man who took notice of you."

"He did so to honor Elimelech and his sons."

"Who remembers my husband and sons?"

"His name is Lord Boaz. Is that familiar?"

"Boaz? Is it possible? He is Elimelech's cousin. The Lord bless him, he is a redeemer, a close relative." Her face brightened. "Did he offer anything for tomorrow?"

Ruth nodded. "He asks that I stay with his women. Maria is another widow with a young son. We helped each other and both came home blessed."

"It is good to remain with his women, under his care. He will not allow any of you to be assaulted, as might happen in another field. Keep close."

"It is indeed an honor. Help me pour the grains and then I will feed the oxen."

"I'll have a light supper for you. It is a good day."

Naomi and Ruth turned the pouch and poured grains into a basket where they could dry. Late afternoon light made long shadows across the courtyard. Ruth skipped. The oxen muttered low tones. She put several handfuls of straw in the trough for them to eat, then hung the bag from a rafter where no one could get into it. Something was stored up there, wrapped in a long dark blanket and forgotten. Ruth tried to pull it down, but only managed dust in her eyes. "Like I didn't get enough of that today," she muttered, using the edge of her skirt to dip into the water trough and wash her face. Then she had to laugh at herself, looking at the dirt-stained linen fabric. "That's not going to help much, is it?"

59

Chapter Eser (ten)

Memory walked beside Naomi as she turned into the high street leading toward the markets of Bethlehem. Boys brandished sticks like swords, swatting at one another, until an old man on the corner grabbed them up in his arms, growling. Their startled yells soon turned to laughter and shrieks as he bounced them up the remainder of the hill. Naomi paused, heart beating swiftly and knees aching. She sighed. This was easier fifteen years ago. After a breather, she continued. She'd barely passed the first shop when a woman cried out and wrapped arms around her.

"I heard talk but didn't dare believe until I had seen you myself."

Naomi smiled as she recognized her. "Zirre. You look the same as when I left."

Zirre held Naomi's arms as she stepped back. Her eyes brightened with tears. "It is you. I have hoped and prayed YHWH would bring this day."

"I am Mara, woman of sorrow. YHWH has not done this for me."

Zirre grasped Naomi's hands. "I do not know why YHWH has taken our men, but I believe he has a plan. A plan for good."

"Dormish?"

"Died in the battle against Moab."

"I am sorry."

"He died honorably. Judge Ehud guides us well in the ways of the Lord. Ehud will visit Bethlehem in a few weeks as he makes a spring journey through the southern cities."

"He stayed with Chillion and Orpah on his visit to King Eglon. He is how we first heard the drought had lifted."

"Have tea with me. There is so much I want to hear. They say you brought a girl back with you."

Naomi allowed herself to be talked into a morning treat. The courtyard of olive trees provided shade. A foreigner from the East prepared large silver jugs with brews of tea. Naomi pulled her cup from the travel bag she carried with her and accepted a brew of cinnamon and clove. The exotic scent reminded her of other Easterners she'd met on the King's road.

Zirre laid her cloak on a patch of scrub grass before sitting. Naomi used her shawl. "It is good to see green. These trees barely lived when we left."

"Batya, look whom I have met in the market," Zirre called to a woman buying tea.

Batya took a step, then noticed Naomi. With a frown, she pulled her scarf tight and walked away.

Zirre watched, her mouth open. "What troubles her?"

Naomi grimaced. "Your sister never forgave me for agreeing to marry Elimelech."

"Batya? She married Sewen and they have two boys and a daughter."

"I am pleased for her. I had not known the joys of daughters until my sons married."

"Have they both returned with you?"

"Only Ruth. I convinced Orpah to return to her family so she could make a new marriage. Ruth refused."

"Ruth? That is an odd name."

Naomi nodded. "She is a Moabitess."

"Don't let that be known."

"We will not lie. She has renounced Moab and its gods and declares she will serve YHWH as I serve YHWH."

"Our priest will read of the Torah on the Sabbath. Have her join us."

"I would love to. It has been too long since I have heard the words of the Lord."

"Where is Ruth? You did not bring her to market with you?"

"She gleans in the fields. It is on that purpose I have come. There will be grain to sell."

"I will gladly take what you have to offer. Foreigners buy supplies as they travel toward Gaza or Heliopolis."

Naomi grabbed Zirre's hand. "Thank you, the Lord bless your kindness."

"You are family. Do you think you will have much?"

"Ruth brought home at least an ephah, yesterday."

"That much? I could fill ten urns. How?"

"She found favor with Boaz, Elimelech's kin."

"He is a redeemer."

Naomi nodded. "Perhaps. Elimelech's brother's son is a closer relative, but I know little about him."

"Athor is not a harsh man. He will like the idea of land."

"I'm sure he will visit when he has time. These harvest months are long and weary. I wonder how Ruth gets on today?"

***

Though the sun stood high in the sky, hazy clouds lingered along the horizon. Ruth wiped sweat from her face with the corner of her tunic. "A little rain will be welcome this afternoon."

Maria peered across the fields to be harvested. "As long as it does not disturb the reaping process."

Elway cried. Ruth reached for the baby. "Let me take him for a moment." She lifted him from the straps. He settled in her arms as Maria sat on a rock.

Daniel appeared beside them with a crock of water. Maria and Ruth held cups for him. "Thank you," Ruth took a cool drink then blew softly on Elway. The little boy rocked in her arms.

Maria chuckled. "He may crawl soon and then I will have to find someone to watch."

"Your family?" Daniel asked as he refilled water.

"I have none."

"Perhaps Naomi." Ruth made faces at the baby.

Daniel adjusted the cap on his head. "Lord Boaz invites you to the meal today. The wizends say rain comes later. The meal tent will be set up a few hours early."

Maria stood, turning so Ruth could set Elway against her back. "We must return to work."

"Follow the path of the wagon. They are starting now." He pointed to the gate where a donkey pulled the long wagon.

"Again?" Ruth asked with wonder.

Daniel smiled. "Lord Boaz insists."

The women did not argue. They continued following the reapers until their bags could hold no more. At the barn, a dark-skinned man waved them from the spinners that would separate the barley. "Have your lunch. Your bags will be ready after the meal." He nodded at Ruth. "I will set yours on the donkey."

Ruth smiled. "Maria's mule, not mine."

"We will travel home together," Maria interjected. "Fit all the bags on the beast."

Ruth protested. "You don't have to do that."

Maria hugged Ruth. "I insist."

Ruth chuckled as Elway grabbed hold of her fingers. "Well, it would give me more time with this fellow." She smiled at the man. "Thank you for your help."

He touched his forehead. "The Lord give you grace."

Maria locked arms with Ruth, and they turned toward the tents where the meal had been prepared. Darker clouds were building on the horizon, but the breeze swayed the cloth gently.

Chapter Ehad-Esre (eleven)

"Boaz."

He turned at his friend's calling, stopping so the other man could catch up.

"The Lord bless you this morning." Joshim touched his forehead. "Are you going to listen to the reading?"

"I am."

He grinned. "What luck. My sister will be sitting with the other ladies. She suggests I invite you for supper. There's plenty of food."

"Her offer is kind. I am honored, but I intend to invite my cousin's wife to a meal. I fear they have little after returning from foreign parts."

Joshim slapped Boaz on the shoulder. "Considerate fellow. I see why you are a favorite of hers. I will give her word to invite Naomi, isn't it? With her daughter-in-law."

"I doubt Akiva will want more guests."

"Of course, she will. You know my sister."

Joshim slipped away when they arrived at the town square. Women were seated on one side. Boaz watched Joshim crouch beside Akiva. The woman smiled, caught Boaz' gaze, and gave an imperceptible nod. She glanced around the gathered crowd of women, then made her way to Naomi.

Although the years had not changed her looks very much, Naomi had sadness about her. Even from across the plaza, Boaz could tell. It was a certain drop of her shoulders and a wrinkle between her brows. Naomi shaded her eyes. Boaz couldn't tell what response she gave. He recognized Ruth sitting beside Naomi. As Akiva walked away, he saw Naomi whisper something to Ruth. Both women smiled. Akiva looked pleased as she returned to her seat. Another gaze and nod in his direction. Boaz shifted his gaze from the ladies. The forward action did not endear her to him.

His thoughts strayed to Ruth, but he shook himself. The young women would find a younger man. A close relative, perhaps, if Naomi were to be redeemed. The notion did not please. He turned his attention to the priest taking a seat on a large rock beneath an olive tree. With eyes closed, the priest spoke the words of YHWH recorded by Moses. Boaz focused his attention where it needed to be.

***

Creation. Ruth wondered at the word. How could a god have created all? Why would he? But the priest spoke of YHWH as a living God. The only living God. A garden with roses and tall trees dripping with fruit filled her mind as she continued to listen. What would it be like to walk in such a place? To know Creator intimately, standing side by side? Ruth didn't want to think about the darkness. Mahlon lay in the darkness. She wanted to remain in the sunlight, listening to water gurgle over rocks as it flowed across the garden. Naomi nudged her, and Ruth startled awake. Naomi grinned; a familiar twinkle sparkled in her eye for a moment. Ruth's unease faded.

The story of a flood sounded similar to legends she'd heard in Moab. The priest continued sharing until the sun was overhead. Ruth blinked. "How do I make sense of all we have heard?"

Naomi squeezed her hand. "The priest reads every Sabbath. The more you hear the stories recorded by Father Moses, the easier they will be understood. Here, help me up."

Ruth stood, then helped pull Naomi to her feet. "Where will we have our meal today?"

An aging friend of Naomi, Dayla, joined them. "Are you coming with us to Akiva's? May I walk with you?"

Naomi sighed. "I did not expect so much kindness."

The women kept a leisurely pace across Bethlehem, to the home of their hosts. Though in the city proper, behind the stone wall lining the street, a large garden spread in front of the house. Others wandered around. Dayla waved at someone and left them. Ruth waited beside Naomi as a gentle wind caused sides of the lunching tent to move. Akiva glided to them, grasping Naomi's hands, and touching cheek to cheek in the customary greeting.

"Zirre has told me much about you, I feel we are already fast friends." The woman's smile seemed genuine. She turned to Ruth. "Welcome. I have not had foreigners; I hope you will find our simple meal to your liking."

Ruth bowed. "Thank you for your kind invitation. I have been with Naomi so long her ways are my ways."

"Come, join us." She stepped aside so they could enter the tent.

Naomi led the way toward other women seated at a low table. Ruth made sure Naomi sat comfortably before taking her own place. "To think, a week ago we traveled a road with few comforts."

Naomi gave a soft smile. "Friends and family have a way of lifting the spirit."

"Do you remember most of them?"

Zirre appeared, stretching across the table with a cry of greeting. "My dear, Naomi." They managed a hug and Zirre sat close enough to talk with them both. "You must be Ruth. You are as beautiful on the outside as you must be inside."

Ruth didn't need to respond. Zirre's bright eyes sparkled as she peered at Akiva across the way then back at Naomi. "Our hosts have excellent taste. I think half of Bethlehem may be here today. How did you enjoy the reading this morning? How long has it been?" She squeezed Ruth's hand. "What were your thoughts, dear? You've had time to pick up the language?"

Ruth noticed the pause and answered. "Mahlon made certain myself and Orpah learned. He had hoped to return one day."

Zirre's eyes darkened. "My apologies. It must be hard to speak of him."

Ruth patted her hand. "My memories are sweet, but we have a new life to build."

Naomi blinked, but remained quiet.

"Greetings, cousin." Boaz stood above them, and then crouched between Zirre and Ruth when Naomi made to stand. "Please, you look settled. I just wanted to be sure all is well. Has Athor sent men to the house to fix what you cannot?"

"I have not seen my nephew. The season is busy, and his men should be helping with harvest. He will come when there is time."

Boaz nodded. "A kind assertion."

"My Lord, Boaz," Akiva called as she glided to them.

He stood. "Thank you for your invitation."

"You are always welcome."

He touched his forehead in gratitude of her compliment. "Peace be with you. I will return to the men. Cousin," he smiled at Naomi, "someone will visit this week to attend to the needs of the house. If we have storms these next weeks, you should at least be dry."

"Thank you. I fear thatching roofs is beyond me."

The four women watched him leave. Akiva grinned at them. "He is a good man. Long overdue for a wife and family."

Zirre shrugged. "Considering his parents, I'm not surprised."

Ruth leaned forward. "His parents? Why would they matter?"

Akiva moved on as Zirre explained. "Rahab lived in Jericho, one of the first of the walled cities to fall. She saved the lives of the spies, and instead of dying with her people, she joined with the Tribe of Judah. Boaz is her son." The twinkle was back, and she grinned at Naomi. "Perhaps he will find a foreigner, like his father."

"I hope you don't mean me," Ruth whispered, cheeks heating. "He won't want a young stranger. I am content with Naomi."

Bread with hummus was provided, turning the conversation to foods.

Long shadows of afternoon led them home after thanking Akiva for her generous hospitality. Ruth linked arms with Naomi as they stepped across uneven bricks. "It may take years for me to figure out how to find my way around Bethlehem."

Naomi drew her toward an alley. "Nearly fifteen years and it hasn't changed. I do wonder how I remember the ways."

"Did you live here as a child?"

"I was born in Bethlehem. Ashei taught a group of us girls, including Zirre and her sister Batya."

"Was her sister with us today?"

"No. Batya and I had feelings for the same man. She could not forgive me when my parents announced my betrothal with Elimelech."

"Was that your fault?"

"The heart doesn't always listen to reason."

Ruth glanced both ways of the road led to by the alley. "This is familiar. The fields are at the bottom of the hill, that way."

"Our house is up the hill." They grinned as they walked.

Fourth Week of the Month of Nisan
Chapter Steim-Esre (twelve)

Ruth dangled thread above a fat-bellied kitten

which tumbled over in its attempt to capture the moving target.

"Aren't they adorable!"

Ruth looked up. "Akiva. I did not expect you." She let the kitten roll from her lap and then stood.

Akiva picked up a gray kitten. "They are sweet. You must let me have one when they come of age."

"Their mother is an excellent mouser."

Akiva held her necklace above the kitten, swaying it back and forth. Tiny gray paws reached for her. "This one is alert. I'm sure they will do well."

"I'll let you know when he's ready for a house. Did you come to speak with Naomi?"

"Boaz mentioned you may have need of blankets and sundry. I've brought a wagon and thought you could take what you need."

Ruth pressed a hand against her chest. "You are too kind."

"Not as much as I should be. I hope Boaz takes note."

"Why would that matter?"

Akiva glanced at the ground as color infused her cheeks. "He is a good man."

"But older than you?"

She laughed. "He has maturity, and yet he remains handsome."

Ruth pushed similar thoughts from her mind. "Are you to be wed?"

Her cheeks darkened even more. She coughed. "No. I mean, there is no understanding. He has never spoken for me. My brother is a close friend. Come, let us explore the wagon."

"Naomi will be sorry she missed you."

Akiva threw back the tarp and Ruth blinked. Blankets. Cloth. Cushions. Pottery. "Feathers? I have never seen a plume this large." Ruth lifted a blue feather of about a cubit in length.

"Something we traded with Easterners. Here, let me get these." She lifted small clay pots with lids. "Dates, olives, figs, cormorant. They are good for cooking." She stretched and brought out a black bag. "This is a treat. Just a little. The crystals are salt."

"It is too much," Ruth's eyes widened at the growing pile beneath the overhang by the side door.

"Naomi is an honored mother. You understand."

Once Akiva left, Ruth put the goods away throughout the house. Foods she carried to the kitchen, moving pots to make room. Blankets she put with the beds. The feather plume went to the animal shelter. Kittens swiftly bounced from a hiding place. Amure beat them, pouncing on the end of the feather, and then hovering there as though she'd caught a mouse. Ruth laughed, then her attention went to the mysterious package in the rafters. Using a box to stand on, she was able to reach one corner. The dull covering wrapped around much brighter material. The fabric was soft, made of a tighter weave than anything she'd seen. "Is it a dress or some kind of tunic?" She wondered aloud. "It must have been a pricey garment."

The sound of wheels drawing up to the house pulled Ruth from her exploring. She hurried out to greet Naomi. "I found something hanging in the stable. It must be clothes, something very fancy." She assisted Naomi from the wagon.

Naomi waved to Zirre. "Blessings upon you, dear friend."

Ruth smiled at Zirre, then turned back to Naomi. "How was town?"

"Spring brings many strangers through our region. I heard languages I do not understand. What is it you found?"

"Through here."

Ruth led the way, but Naomi was distracted by the long colorful feather on the ground. "Where did this come from?"

"Mistress Akiva brought useful supplies. Does that look familiar?" Ruth pointed at the light fabric dangling from one end of the package.

"My goodness," Naomi pressed a hand against her chest. "Elimelech bought the fabric before we moved to Moab. When it wasn't in the wagons, I never gave it another thought. To think, it's been wrapped here all these years."

"You can sew a new dress."

Naomi scoffed. "What need has an old woman for a new dress? Leave it for now, I'm sure a purpose for it will come to light." She bent slow but managed to pick up one of the kittens. "They are doing well. What did Akiva bring for us?"

Ruth led the way to the kitchens. Naomi grinned at the porch nearly overflowing with barley. "I'll ask Zirre to take some to dry at her house. The first batches should be dry enough from last week to offer to the priests and then sell."

"Offer to the priests? What will they do with it?"

"The Feast of the First fruits has passed, but I honor YHWH and His bounty by offering what we have to our priests."

"Will they burn it like the other sacrifices?"

"They will more likely cook with it. Their job is to do the bidding of YHWH. It is my pleasure to help them."

Ruth wrapped her arm around Naomi. "Then it is my pleasure as well."

Chapter Shlosh-Esre (thirteen)

Maria wiped her forehead with a corner of her skirt. "I don't remember days getting this hot so early in the season."

Ruth adjusted the bag she carried to fill easier. "Have you gleaned like this before?"

Maria's shoulders drooped. "Bonem worked as a reaper. There was no need for me to work the fields as well."

"You have no family to help?"

She shook her head. "My parents died. I was their only child. I have a cousin, but he has eleven children as it is. I have no desire to seek a corner among so many." She paused with a handful of barley. "Why didn't you return to your family?"

"Mother died when I was young, before she could provide sons. Having a daughter was hard for my father. Naomi became my mother. I couldn't imagine leaving her."

"I hope I can meet her."

"Join us for an evening meal. We have guests nearly every night. We'll sit around the fire and tell stories. An elder mistress told us of the first man and woman. They had two sons."

Maria nodded and resumed collecting grains. "Cain

and Abel. The story reminds us how easily we can lose our way."

"Do you believe the stories of Father Moses?" Ruth set her bag beside a large pile of barley. "Here, we can split this."

"There are elders who remember him."

"They must be very old."

Maria grinned. "Ancient, though not as old as the people before the flood. Father Moses is revered. His face shone like sunlight when he talked with YHWH. They made him wear a veil. He wrote a book of history. How could he have learned such details but from YHWH Himself?"

Elway began to cry. Ruth brushed hair from his forehead. "He's warm. Take him to the shade. Be sure he has water. I'll continue to gather and share with you."

"I can't do that."

"You will." Ruth handed the baby a thick stalk to chew. "Let him cool down. I'll meet you at the lunch tent."

Maria sighed, but the fussy child needed tending. "I will make it up to you."

"Your friendship has been a balm to my soul. There is nothing to make up." Ruth continued in the field. A short time later, she noticed the supervisor, Daniel, offering Maria and Elway water. His next move brought him to Ruth.

"The air is hot and heavy today. I thought I would bring water for all."

"You are kind." Ruth drew her metal cup from a pocket in her skirt. The cool water refreshed, easing the dryness of her throat. "Thank you."

Daniel set the water bucket on the ground and reached

for Ruth's bag. "Maria says you intend to share your gleaning. Allow me to help." He held the bag open, making it easier for Ruth to add grains.

His unexpected gesture held her silent. She scooped up a bundle and added it to the bag.

"Have you known Mistress Maria long?" Daniel shook the bag to make more room.

"Only since moving here. She became my guide the first day. Her son, Elway, brightens each hour we work."

Daniel's cheeks seemed to darken, though perhaps the sun caused it. "Does she speak often of her husband?"

Ruth shook her head, hiding a smile. "Only that he was killed in battle against Moab. I thought my parentage would make her hate me, but she demonstrates friendship and honor. She is a good woman."

"Bonem was a close friend. Their marriage was decided by their families, but they seemed pleased with the choice."

"It must have been hard losing him. Does your culture have a period of mourning before she considers a different marriage?"

"Mourning tends to be a month or longer. Sometimes the heart does not let go."

Ruth filled the last space in the bag. "If you add more grains, I won't be capable of carrying it."

"I will leave this at the thresher. The lunch tent will be set up. You can fill Maria's bag once we have eaten."

Ruth nodded. "Your kindness overwhelms. I pray you have much success."

Without the burden of her gleaning bag, Ruth crossed to the tents quickly. She took a seat beside Maria. At first, she thought Maria's lack of conversation was her focus on Elway. "May I share bread? Has the break cooled him?"

Maria's eyes gleamed hard. "We are rested." She moved the bread to where Ruth could reach for it.

Ruth frowned. "Has something happened? No one bothered you?"

Maria jabbed bread in a sesame sauce. "The supervisor seemed intent on helping you."

"I'm glad he carried my bag to the threshers. I'm not sure I could have. We'll be able to fill your satchel after lunch."

"No need for that."

Ruth tilted her head. "Do you not like Daniel? I thought…"

Maria interrupted with a glare. "He seems more interested in you."

"Me? He wasn't asking questions about me."

"What do you mean?"

Ruth plopped a date in her mouth. "He asked about you."

Maria looked down at her plate, cheeks reddening. "About me?"

"Yes, you. He's obviously interested. You really thought he would look twice at a foreigner like me?"

"You're beautiful and caring. More than half the overseers would try something if Lord Boaz didn't keep them in check."

"I think you are mistaken." It was Ruth's turn to feel heat in her face. She brushed back a wisp of hair. "Are you ready to return to the field?"

They both looked at Elway who grappled with a bit of cloth. His legs jerked back and forth. Maria wrapped the carrier around him then settled him against her back. Ruth draped fabric around his head.

***

"Serena, you are a welcome surprise," Naomi wiped her hands on her apron before welcoming the woman with a hug.

Serena stepped around rocks Naomi used to border a garden at the side of the house. "Let me help you."

"Surely, you don't need to crawl around in the dirt." A man's voice interrupted.

The women turned, both shading their eyes to see. Serena frowned. "Hador? Why are you here?"

"I had business with Risyln and decided to check in on my cousin." He looked at Naomi.

Naomi lifted her brows. "Me? I do not know you."

"I'm Helena's son. I've kept my eye on the property. It isn't as run down as expected."

"Thank you for your kindness. Elimelech's family will be grateful."

He waved. "What need do they have for a bit like this?"

Naomi cleared her throat, but Hador interrupted before she could respond. "We don't need to discuss business today. You have chosen well for a kitchen garden. Perhaps when plants have ripened to harvest, we may have a meal together." With a nod, he wandered away.

Naomi watched him leave with a puzzled look. "Why does he think this property would be available to him?"

"Perhaps he does not know Elimelech's family?" Serena shrugged. "But he has lived in Bethlehem his entire life. He should not be surprised." She helped clear a section of the garden. With the plot prepared, she stood beside Naomi on one end. "Let us visit my home. There are plenty of plants to share now the drought has ended.

"I have a few seeds in a jar in the cooking room."

Serena nodded. "Both will fill the garden. Do you have a basket?"

Naomi consented. In a matter of minutes, she had a basket balanced on her head as they walked the lane toward the westside of Bethlehem. The rocky outcrop bordering town followed the lane.

"These caves are new." Naomi peered into one of the dark openings.

"Boaz encouraged travelers to visit. The Inn's needed stables. Much of the rock they were able to crush and mix into clay."

"To make bricks?"

Serena shook her head. "For pottery. He's also brought carpenters. Travelers pay with food and stores. It has been a help to many."

"Your family chose wisely."

Easy chatter followed them across Bethlehem. The rocky border became more of a fence overlooking fields. Naomi smiled. "Of course, Rahab's home. I remember it well." Though the shape was the same as her own, three sides around a courtyard, the home of Salmon and Rahab was larger.

"Mother Rahab passed a few years ago. Boaz has the main building. The families of Arron and Leti have the middle portion."

"The Jericho twins? They must be old."

"Ancient." Serena grinned. "But they refuse to believe it."

"What of their children?"

"Ahmon and Cush, their families are here. Roon died, the same sickness that took Father Salmon."

"Losing sons is a bitter wound."

"It is good to have much family around. Now that you have returned, perhaps family can ease the hurt you suffer." Serena squeezed Naomi's hand. "The gardens are over here." She led Naomi from the courtyard, through a breezeway, and past an outdoor oven.

Naomi allowed herself to be led, thankful not to reply. The weight on her heart was too close to speak without tears. The garden had a perfect spot between the house and the rocky edge of the mountain. Two gnarled olive trees provided shade on the far side, otherwise, the garden basked in the sun.

"We have lots of little tomato plants. The greens will be easy to replant. We can try the potatoes and sweets, not sure how they will manage." Serena nabbed a tool from the house, and before long, Naomi filled the basket.

"I don't think anymore will fit." The smell of plants and rich soil permeated the warm afternoon.

"I'll have Talia lead the donkey. This will be too heavy to carry on its own."

"You don't have to do that."

Serena laid a hand on Naomi's shoulder. "It will be my pleasure. We'll have a light meal. By the time we return to your place, Talia will have the garden ready to plant."

"Then you will join us for supper. I have stew simmering. Ruth brought lamb meat home with her yesterday."

"Here is Talia," Serena greeted the young woman.

"Ahlan wa sahlan." Talia bounced down the stairs to join them.

Serena shook her head. "Save your languages for the marketplace." She turned to Naomi. "Talia has a gift. Sometimes, it seems she hears strangers talking and before long, she's able to join in."

"Is she your daughter?" Naomi asked as she helped Talia hook the basket to a donkey.

"I am not married. She is my cousin. Father Salmon's closest friend married Elia, his sister. Talia is the daughter of their son."

The young woman scratched the tawny beast between the ears. "I'll wait for you at Mistress Naomi's?"

"Would you like to take a bar with you?" Naomi held the tray toward her. The young woman grabbed two, then pushed on the donkey to get him started.

Serena led Naomi to a bench overlooking the garden. "Workers delivered fresh wine yesterday. I'll bring you some."

The light taste of grape renewed Naomi. "We should walk back, or I may decide to rest a while. The garden is very pleasant."

Serena agreed. "I like to sit in the evenings when the birds call."

The walk seemed easier, not only because she carried nothing on her head, but much of the way was flat or downhill.

"Should I tell Boaz of Hador's words?" Serena asked as they turned the corner to Naomi's home.

"I don't see why, now Hador knows Elimelech's relations are near."

Talia skipped across the yard to greet them. "I laid plants in the plot. I can dig them in if you'd like."

"You've done more than enough," Naomi protested and looked at Serena. "Both of you. I thank YHWH for your kindness."

Talia grinned. "If I'm here helping you, I don't have to sit and sew."

Serena bumped her shoulder. "Sewing is an important skill to learn for a woman."

"Not when I poke my finger more than the fabric."

Serena smiled. "You'll have plenty of time for lessons even after planting."

Naomi shrugged. "Your arrangement seems fine. Let us plant."

86

Chapter Arba-esre (fourteen)

The next day, Ruth left early for another day of harvesting as Naomi gathered a few items to take into the city. She was straightening a jar in the small wagon when someone pulled up to her house. She leaned against the wagon, shielding her eyes from the sun as a man halted his donkey.

"Hello, ma'am." Daniel nabbed his hat from his head as he nodded. "I'm a foreman for Lord Boaz. He's sent me to check on the condition of your roof. And anything else that may catch my attention."

Naomi tilted her head. "Lord Boaz? I thought Athor would be the one to take care of matters."

"I saw the two of them talking."

"I appreciate your assistance, whomever has sent you. I'm taking the little cart to market. You won't need me here?"

"Not at all. It's a fine day for the bazaar. Are you taking up a load of the barley?"

"Yes. Lord Boaz has blessed us."

"He is a good man. Don't take less than what it's worth. Some of those travelers will haggle till they wear you down."

"Zirre agreed to assist. We are old friends."

"Mrs. Garver? Her husband was my uncle."

"I never knew him well."

"He was decent enough, though I think he lived a bit in her shadow."

Naomi laughed. "She does have a way of grabbing attention. Suits her since she is a merchant. Thank you for your help."

"I'll bring the wagon around with your ox."

"You don't need to do that."

"Please," he stepped back and put his hat on. "Pulling an ox makes me thankful for the donkey I have."

Naomi pointed at the rafters. "Since you're heading that way. There's a bundle of fabric up there. Could you take it down and place it by my bed upstairs?"

"Of course." He nodded, then went to grab the leads of the ox. The animal gave no protest, and Naomi was on her way in a matter of minutes.

***

Everyone gladly sought the lunch tent as early as possible. Maria glanced around. "I have not seen Daniel today."

"Or Lord Boaz," Ruth added as she filled a cup with fresh water.

"Heat like this usually leads to rain. I hope we finish most of the harvest of barley before too much water ruins the plants."

Ruth agreed as she dipped bread in a vinegar oil. Elway gurgled in his sleep and both women smiled down on him. "He's such a good baby."

Maria agreed.

A tall, thin man moved to their table. He placed a bag in front of Ruth. "Lord Boaz wanted to be sure a meal was sent home with you. My wife has cured lamb. Her garden yielded early onions. If you plant the few that are here, you'll have more for the fall."

"Thank you." Ruth accepted the gift. "Where has Lord Boaz gone?"

The man shrugged. "He has travelled from the region."

***

"Lord Boaz."

Boaz turned at the sound of his name. A younger man with a friendly smile waived. "Athor." Boaz stepped off the path so others in the crowded market could continue their way. "What brings you to Hommish?"

Athor drew closer. "I ordered a special gift when Norsin last stayed in Bethlehem. I received word he was near and had finished." He drew a pouch from an inner pocket. As he tossed back the edge of skin, lapis sparkled in the sun. The string of beads had many shades of blue, from the deep lapis to pale topaz.

"Remarkable. It cannot be for your mother."

Athor swallowed. "I have someone else in mind."

Boaz grinned. "You mean to engage yourself to someone? Who is she?"

"Diane, the daughter of the sheep herder."

Boaz nodded. "Jesseth? Seems a good man, though he came to Bethlehem only a year ago. I don't think I've seen him with a daughter."

"She is fair and lovely, no matter how plain her father may be." He wrapped the necklace with care and returned it to his pocket. "You mustn't say anything. I intend to set up our home before I speak with her father."

"If she is of marrying age, you may want to tell him sooner."

"We'll see. What brings you to Hommish?"

"I came to barter the price of grains. Travelers along

the highway have connections to Egypt or the far East."

Athor grimaced. "I should have paid closer attention to your business. I'm afraid I don't have the same mind for it."

"Spend time with the Elders in the gates of Bethlehem. You'll learn what manner of business suits you."

The cousins parted ways. Boaz chose an inn near the marketplace.

***

Quiet settled around Naomi once she returned from the city. With the others gone, she perched on a bench in the garden, leaning against the stone wall. Laughter tickled her memory. Chillion leaned through the upper window. Mahlon, taller and older of the two, held a ball beyond Chillion's reach. He'd tossed it to Naomi. Bright eyes of Chillion flashed and then both boys disappeared, though the sound of their feet running down the stairs thudded across the yard. Naomi glanced at the arched opening into the garden, expecting to see the boys coming for their toy. But her hands were empty, and only the cry of birds feeding in bright afternoon interrupted the silence.

"I imagine you see loved ones in the shadows."

A familiar voice startled Naomi from her reverie. "The Lord bless you. What brings you this far from the city? Did I leave something behind?" She started to stand, but Zirre waved her to remain seated.

"I heard something since you left. You're selling property to Hador? Are you planning to leave again?"

Naomi frowned. "I told Hador Elimelech has close relatives. They are both his brother's and cousins' families."

Zirre hugged Naomi. "So, you aren't leaving? I just got you back."

"Come inside. I have a few tea leaves. We can sit and enjoy a cup together."

"Sounds lovely. Perhaps we can plot how to thwart Hador's plans."

Naomi shook her head as she stoked the fire and placed a pan with water to heat. She added half the remaining leaves. "What does he think he can do?"

"He holds no regard for women. Elimelech's family needs to speak up for you."

"Isn't Judge Ehud traveling this way soon? I can bring the matter before him."

Zirre nodded. "He is a fair man, even if he uses the wrong hand. I heard that's how he managed to kill King Eglon. No one suspected he carried a sword because it was on the wrong side."

"I never saw it." Naomi turned to grab two mugs for the heated drink.

Zirre leaned forward. "You saw Judge Ehud in Moab?"

"We had dinner together," she said with a nod. She placed drinks on the table then took a moment to sit on the bench across from Zirre. "Well-spoken and personable. I can see why he was permitted an audience with the king."

"Was King Eglon as fat as they say?"

Naomi laughed. "Enormous. A good foot taller than my boys and wider than the two of them standing side by side." Her eyes darkened. "They wanted to fight, but they'd grown up with the Moabites in our village. They couldn't imagine meeting any of them in battle." She wiped a tear from her eye. "Is that why they died?

YHWH punished them? He punished me for not bringing them back to Bethlehem when Elimelech died."

Zirre grabbed Naomi's hand. "I don't know why your boys died, and we don't know yet if something good can come of all this." She thought for a moment, then asked, "Where would Ruth be without you and your son?"

Naomi dabbed her eyes once more. "She is a dear girl. Her father did not treat her kindly. I don't know, how can there be any special purpose in Ruth coming to Bethlehem?"

"That is a question I cannot answer. We have to wait and see."

First Week of the Month of Iyar
Chapter Hanesh-esre (fifteen)

"What do you think of Bethlehem? Have you traveled our land?"

"I have only seen what lies between Naomi's house and the fields." Ruth tried to keep her focus on the plain cloth covering the table, but she couldn't seem to stop stealing glances of Boaz. "And into town with your sister."

"Today finishes the barley harvest and we are still a few weeks from wheat. I can show you around. There are markets to sell grains you have collected. Bakeries that can use your meal, even some of the ale houses."

"I am astonished you would have time."

"I have vendors to meet as well."

Ruth took a breath. "I would be honored. When would be a useful time for you?"

"Tomorrow. Early, we should be able to meet with many of the shop owners. Then, there are other places to see, if the weather holds."

"Shall I meet you at the gate?" At his agreement, Ruth tried to keep excitement at bay. He was an elder, there was no purpose in thinking of him as anything else.

Morning rose with a mist to shroud the light. Ruth laced her leather shoes as Naomi sipped a cup of tea.

"Lord Boaz is a keen businessman. He will guide you well for what we have." Naomi made Ruth recite the list of goods they would have to sell.

Boaz met her as she turned onto the avenue leading to the gates. They started the uphill climb to the main city gate. Ruth leaned across a wall built at the edge of the drop. "Who chose to build Bethlehem among the hills? Wouldn't it have been easier in the flat lands?"

"Ah, you must remember, this land was filled with many city-states not so long ago, before Father Joshua and our people regained the lands of Father Abraham. The hills provide advantage over others in this region." They resumed the climb. Boaz bowed to several elders sitting along the gate.

An older man with grayish-green head cloths waved at them. "Lord Boaz, may we have your assistance with today's business?"

Boaz lifted his hand in greeting. "My apologies, I am on errand. I will gladly sit with you in the afternoon tomorrow."

"A sound plan." He nodded. "We look forward to your insight."

Ruth kept her head down until they passed through the arch of stone. "I see many of the same elders there every day."

"They support the needs of our community. When there are disputes or business to be settled, if an agreement can be reached, we will make the necessary motions to do so."

"What if the business cannot be settled?"

"As a nation, we have a judge with whom we may appeal. His decision does not require consent. Here is a more direct route to the upper markets." Boaz motioned to an alley on the right.

Smaller cobbles covered the narrower road. On both sides, stone and brick formed the row of houses. Archways led into courtyards. Short balconies hung above them. The way was steep, but at the end, the path opened, and they were in the market.

Boaz proved his words. Ruth greeted an honest ale man. The men shook hands at a fair deal for malt. Zirre assured them none other could provide the prices she could for barley wheat, bricks, and fodder. Boaz laughed at her insistence.

The sun had not yet reached midmorning as they crossed the highroad and walked the street in the oldest part of the city. As they passed the cluster of buildings, the road opened, heading in a southeasterly direction. Short grasses and scrub brush covered rolling hills. Darker mountains, not the great mountains, rose in the distance.

"It's beautiful." Ruth stood by a stone wall.

"The day is early enough. We can walk a distance. I'll have my servants meet up to us with lunch." At Ruth's consent, he went to make the arrangements.

***

"What is this place?" Ruth kept her head covered even though a tree growing among the hills offered shade from the overhead sun. A breeze drifted past them, and the hush was as though an elder stood nearby. Her voice sounded as small as she felt.

"Father Israel buried his wife, Rachel."

Ruth studied the silent hills. "The wife he loved? Serena shared their story."

Boaz leaned against the curved trunk of the tree. "We have many stories to tell. Moses did well to write of his

Patriarchs. Joshua did too."

"Is there one who makes record of these days?"

"Who can tell? Who can make sense of the struggles we have with the remnants of Canaan?"

"Perhaps one day."

"It would take a wise man to see all that has been and what it means." Boaz smiled at Ruth. "I am not that wise."

Ruth searched the Judean mountains in the distance. "Have you crossed the mountains?"

Boaz shuddered. "I prefer the desert Negev to the south, or the sea. There are ships to carry goods around our world. As long as storms do not interfere, we are more likely to have goods arrive safely by ship than across mountains."

"We traveled the King's Highway from Moab. Many strange people follow that path."

"I have never been through Moab."

She laughed. "You would recognize it. There are hills, but no mountains. Crops will grow across the fields. Workers cluster in villages while larger cities..." She shook her head. "Not really sure what goes on in larger cities."

"Maybe you will be able to visit Jerusalem one day."

She chuckled. "I would get lost in Jerusalem. Bethlehem is big enough."

Boaz motioned for them to continue. A servant tapped a donkey and followed with the remains of lunch as they took a trail leading back to the city. "Your village was smaller than Bethlehem?"

"One main street. A few farmer shops, though most everyone traveled to Al-karak for market days."

"Our two market districts work well enough. The high

road catches those from the King's Road while the low street works for others heading toward the coast."

Ruth pondered the remains of the day as she curled on a bench in the garden. Boaz had escorted her home. The servant placed leftover goods in the kitchen area, including a bottle of wine. Roasted lamb meat would pair well with tabbouleh salad made from soaked barley grains.

"We will need to make bread tomorrow," Naomi said as she handed Ruth a cup of hot tea. She sat on a bench across from her daughter-in-law. "I was thinking we could trade an ephah of grain for some honey."

"Rosemary has grown enough we could add some also." Ruth suggested. "I'll grind the flour while you shop for honey."

"You don't have to do that."

"We are between harvests. I can help take care of the house."

Their conversation turned to a discussion on herbs and how well they grew compared to Moab.

***

There were enough chores around the house to keep busy for the week. Several times they took shopping trips into Bethlehem. Bread baking on more than one occasion. Naomi tried to get Ruth to help with collecting honey, but a sting on her arm sent her swiftly on a different errand. She woke early on Sabbath.

"Ye shall be holy for I the Lord your God am holy." The words spoken by the priest remained with Ruth as she and Naomi joined Zirre for an afternoon meal. Batya sulked on the far side of the table while her husband, Sewen, stood with the men in the garden.

"You are quiet today." Zirre smiled at Ruth.

"The gods of Moab were never considered holy. What makes YHWH holy?"

Naomi broke from the loaf of bread in the middle of the table. "Do you remember the first of the commandments given to Father Moses?"

Ruth tilted her head as she thought a moment. "Thou shalt have no other gods before me."

"Very good. He can say that because He is the beginning of all things. What He makes holy is holy."

Batya moved closer with a frown. "It is not your place to teach such things. There are men and priests."

Naomi shook her head. "I lived fifteen years in a foreign land. After Elimelech died, how could my sons learn of our ways unless I taught them?"

"You see what your sin has brought you."

Zirre gasped. "Batya! Such a horrid thing to say."

Batya glared at her sister's reprimand but left without further comment.

Naomi blinked. "I never thought…"

Zirre grabbed her hand. "So, don't. Have faith like we've seen in Mother Sarah or Mother Rachel. They made mistakes yet they were blessed by YHWH. Your way will be blessed as well."

Ruth held Naomi's other hand. "If He can take me in as a child of Israel, there is sure hope for you."

Second Week of the Month of Iyar
Chapter Shesh-esre (sixteen)

Ruth sat beside Naomi as morning sun danced through the thickening leaves in the trees outside the window. A hint of sweet tarried on the breeze.

Naomi didn't seem as enamored of the view. "Judge Ehud will be visiting Bethlehem this week."

"What is the significance of that?"

"Hador wants to take the field. He has no right to it. The matter can be brought to Master Ehud to judge."

Ruth shifted toward Naomi. "Can you stand against him?"

"I will speak with Lord Boaz. He has been generous and kind. I pray he will be willing to help with the matter."

"We have not yet moved to the wheat fields now that barley is harvested. Still, they set up the meal tents for those working in the barns. He usually comes with the meal."

Naomi raised one brow. "You noticed his comings and goings?"

She laughed. "He invited the gleaners to eat in the tent daily."

"He is not a bad choice, even if he is older than you."

Ruth gazed at the floor, slight color in her cheeks. "I

am a foreign widow. I doubt a Lord of Bethlehem thinks more of me than a poor relative."

Naomi sighed. "Can I trust YHWH to have a plan and purpose in this? Dare I trust?"

"The stories the elders share, haven't good things come even from the worst of circumstance?"

Naomi grabbed Ruth's hands and smiled. "You are proof of that." She took a breath. "Perhaps there is good that can yet come. I will seek Lord Boaz."

"Should I come with you?"

"No," Naomi said as she leaned back. "You already have plans to mix the malt barrels and then take another load of dried barley to Zirre. She'll need your help with the miller."

"She said they have a system of stones. I am curious to see."

"Then go. I will find Lord Boaz."

***

A walking stick helped Naomi along the uneven path toward the fields, but her determination was rewarded. A wagon with a large black horse rumbled nearby. She recognized Boaz walking behind. She waved, and he motioned at his servant to stop the wagon.

"Mistress Naomi, the Lord bless you this morning."

She nodded at his gracious greeting, then swallowed. "May I have a word?"

Boaz waved at his servants. "Set things in place. I will meet you there." The cart rolled on as Boaz invited Naomi to sit on the short wall beneath a myrtle tree. "How may I be of service?"

Naomi pressed her hands together. "You have been very kind since my return to Bethlehem. You honor me and Ruth with your generosity."

"Elimelech befriended me in my youth. Any honor is from him."

Naomi took a breath. "Then I hope this will not seem untoward. Do you know Hador?"

His face darkened. "More than I care too."

"He has tried to lay claim to the field that belongs with our house."

"Claim? What claim does he have?"

She rolled her eyes. "He doesn't have to speak to me, a woman. I desire to bring him to Judge Ehud. Let him decide."

"Hador has no claim to redeem. Does he mean to have Ruth as well?"

Though the question seemed innocent, Naomi noticed a momentary look of concern and her heart lightened. "As you say, he is no redeemer. I do not think Ruth would appreciate him."

"You know her well?"

Her smile softened. "Even before Mahlon married her, she became a daughter to me. She is the sort of woman who will not abandon those she loves deeply. She is kindness itself yet dragged me with her when I lost the desire to continue."

Boaz squeezed her hand. "I am thankful she has been good to you. I will speak with Hador, and I will stand for you in the court of the judge."

Naomi closed her eyes and took a deep breath. When she opened them, her heart felt calm. "Thank you."

***

The court of the judge was a long low building beside the town square. Though Ehud had arrived the evening before, it was on the morning of Shlishi, the third day of the week, that the square filled with people of the region come to settle conflicts. A system of lottery gave order to the crowd. Boaz watched Hador select a stone. Rather than select one of his own, he waited for Hador's appointment with Judge Ehud. Hador took no notice of Boaz following him into the court. Ehud sat in a wood-carved chair. Near him were two priests, scribes by the look of the scrolls spread on a short table. Hador rubbed his hands together as he approached.

"What issue do you bring forward to judge?" Ehud crossed one leg over the other.

Hador nodded. "If it please you, your servant seeks the ownership of a field on the outskirts of Bethlehem."

"Have you made inquiry with the owner?"

"Elimelech is dead. His sons as well. There are none who remain to claim it."

"Seems an easy decision to make."

Boaz moved forward. "Judge Ehud. I am Lord Boaz, of the house of Judah. I come on behalf of the family to negate Hador's claim."

Ehud frowned. "Family?" He glanced at Hador. "I thought you said they were dead."

Hador opened his mouth, but Boaz stepped nearer. "It is true, Elimelech and his two sons died in Moab. You met the sons, I believe. Mahlon and Chillion?"

"Before the battle of Moab. Of course, I was a guest in the home of Chillion and his wife."

"Then you met Naomi as well?"

"The mother?" He nodded. "We enjoyed conversation."

"Naomi and her daughter-in-law Ruth live in the house that goes with the field. They are not without protection." Boaz glared at Hador. "Athor is Elimelech's nephew and I am his cousin."

"There are redeemers for Naomi?" At Boaz' nod, Ehud struck a small bell. The priest lifted a seal. Notes were scribed on the page and then hot wax dripped on it. The priest pressed the seal into the wax, leaving an impression.

Hador frowned. "What does that mean?"

Ehud motioned for a guard to call the next appointment. He frowned at Hador. "The property you seek is not within your grasp. There are others to preserve it for the seed of Elimelech."

Hador stuttered. "If they were going to make that claim, shouldn't they have done so?"

Ehud looked to Boaz. Boaz nodded. "Our servants have fixed the home where Naomi now lives, though the house stood empty for fifteen years. Naomi and her daughter-in-law are under my protection. Athor has yet to decide. If he does or does not," Boaz glared at Hador, "the women remain in my protection."

Ehud smiled. "The matter is settled. I have many more issues to address, thank you sirs."

Although Hador tried to engage him in conversation, Boaz grinned as he left the court and turned toward the fields. The other man did not intend to give up so easily.

"Your lands do well, I believe," Hador interrupted, huffing as he lengthened his stride to keep up with Boaz. "What need have you for another?"

"The land is for Naomi, to do with as she pleases."

"And for her daughter-in-law, the Moabitess? I did not want to say anything. What might Ehud do knowing an enemy was near?"

"Mistress Ruth has aligned herself with YHWH. She is no enemy."

He stammered. "Of course, I know that. I've

considered wedding her. I think she would approve."

"Marrying you?" Boaz scoffed.

"That is why I sought the field. Once that was in my possession, I would have something worth making an offer." When Boaz remained quiet, he continued. "You aren't young. You forget what it's like for a heart to beat for another."

"I am not a dodder. As I've said, she remains under my protection. Naomi and Ruth remain under my protection." Boaz stopped and peered at Hador. The younger man frowned but said nothing more. He finally turned onto a side road and Boaz continued on the high street. Still, something in Hador's words stung.

Chapter Sheva-esre (seventeen)

The week was passing. Ruth noticed Naomi's glances toward the window throughout the morning. She paused in her chores to share water with her. "Go, visit with your friend." Ruth handed Naomi a woven wrap. "I believe some of the fruits have ripened enough to pick. I also need to turn drying grains."

Naomi squeezed Ruth's hands. "There will not be many days between the barley and wheat harvests."

"I enjoy the garden. So much has come to life. It is not barren as when we first arrived."

When Naomi continued to hesitate, Ruth laughed and pushed her from the house.

When she was finally on her way, Ruth pulled a long-handled tool with a metal end for scraping in the soil. Birds chatted around her as she loosened a patch to check on potatoes.

"Seems like the ground here is as fertile as the field beyond."

Ruth jumped, startled by the stranger's voice. She whirled around with the digging tool braced in her hands. "I did not realize anyone was here."

He nodded. "I'm an old family friend. Hador."

She frowned. "Hador? The one who tried to take Naomi's property?"

"She is old, she has no use for the field," he waved off her indignation. "You should be looking for protection for yourself."

"My place is with Naomi. You should leave."

He took a step closer. "You don't need me to leave yet."

Ruth straightened. "You forget. I've been married. I know where to hit a man to make him hurt." She tightened her hands on the garden tool.

Hador backed up.

"Am I interrupting?" Boaz appeared from around the corner. His face darkened as he glanced at Hador.

Ruth breathed. "He came to enquire and has been told he is not welcome."

Hador's face twisted as he scowled at Ruth. "You are a foreigner. You'll bring curses on us."

"I have cleaved unto Naomi and sworn that her God is my God."

Boaz crossed his arms. Though Hador was younger, Boaz' height and thick shoulders overshadowed the other man. Hador turned with a grunt and disappeared. Ruth smiled at Boaz. "I do not understand men who would use force to get their way." She returned to digging up potatoes.

"Mahlon wasn't that way, was he?"

"Oh, no. He was always kind. Mischievous, especially if it meant outdoing his brother."

"Then who?" Boaz brought a basket and gathered the loosened potatoes, shaking dirt from them before laying inside.

Ruth stopped. Looking at Boaz, she could never imagine him lifting a hand to hurt. "My father." She surprised herself by blurting out. "Mother died soon after

I was born so he could never have a son. He was not pleased."

"I'm sorry."

"Naomi showed me what it means to have a mother. I could never leave her." She cleared her throat. "Did you need something?"

"I came to tell you wheat harvesting will begin next week. Let your friend, Maria, know as well. My overseer will give direction on what to do."

"Thank you for your kindness."

He left shortly after. Ruth stood, leaning against the garden tool, watching where he'd been. A bird called. She shook herself and returned to the potatoes.

Week 3 of the Month of Iyar
Chapter Shmona-esre (eighteen)

The sun peeked above the horizon to the East as Ruth turned the corner toward the far fields ripe with wheat. Golden light touched the plants as the last breath of night moved through. A line of reapers stood within a stone ring. Ruth slowed until she noticed other gleaners. Elway recognized her; his chubby legs kicked against his mother's back. Maria turned with a smile.

"Good morning, friend." She moved closer. "How are you?"

Ruth grinned. "We have a garden now. You'll come see?"

"I have a few things growing outside the kitchen but would be helpful to see a full garden. What do you have there?"

Ruth lowered her basket. "Naomi discovered clothes from the boys. They are still good. She thought to donate them to the priest to share as needed." She lifted a wrapped package from the top of the pile. "Here, I gathered some items for Elway. I also brought blankets to cover the rocks so he can crawl while we eat our meal."

"You are a blessing. If you take the others to the tent, I'm sure Lord Boaz will have one of the overseers deliver them to the priest."

It was a better plan than trying to keep dirt and plants out of the basket as they worked. Ruth hurried across the field. Her heart thudded as she caught sight of Boaz.

"Lord Boaz," a woman called from the lane.

He turned, frowning. "Akiva? Why have you come?"

Ruth halted beside the tent, basket in her arms. She meant to turn aside but found herself listening.

Akiva lifted a wide, shallow bowl. "Joshim's traders gave him a treat from the far East. We thought to share it with your workers."

"Joshim should have brought it. You do not belong here."

Akiva placed the bowl on the table. "There are women in the fields."

"They have a purpose which you do not. Go home."

She left the bowl. "May the sun grace your day." She bowed and turned.

Ruth closed her eyes. Why wasn't Akiva's place at the field? Because she wasn't poor and needy as the other women who followed the reapers? She took a breath.

"Ruth?" Akiva noticed the other woman as she tugged a harness on the donkey pulling a small cart.

Ruth gripped the basket tighter. "The Lord bless you," she greeted.

Akiva smiled, though her eyes did not gleam bright as usual. "Do you need help?"

She shook her head. "Maria's baby Elway is crawling. I brought blankets for the area where we eat to protect him from the rocks. You don't mind if they are used in this manner?"

"Of course not." Akiva assured. "It must be difficult to work in the field with her child."

"He is a good boy. Seems to enjoy moving."

Boaz stood in the corner of the tent, watching as Ruth placed the blankets near the pen Daniel had formed. Ruth set the basket beside a rock. "Naomi found clothes from her boys when they were little. The fabric is still good. She thought to share them." She gave a shy smile and a slight bow.

"I'll have Daniel take them to the priest. Let Naomi know we appreciate her kindness."

Ruth wanted to invite him to thank her in person, but words stuck in her throat. "I should return to work."

Boaz watched her leave.

***

Ruth crossed through the field to catch up with Maria. Wheat brushed against her arms, not quite as prickly as the barley with its long wisps. Maria handed her a bag. "Daniel said to follow the reapers."

It did not take long to fall back into the rhythm of collecting the cut plant material. Men brought water as the day warmed. Ruth wiped sweat from her face and neck as she stretched. Her feet dragged by the time they were welcomed to eat the meal.

Lord Boaz met them there. Ruth glanced at him as she washed her hands. She pulled Elway from the carrier and held him as Maria washed his face and feet. They entered the tent. Ruth slowed as she noticed the head table set beside the pen where Elway could crawl. Boaz invited them to sit.

Once food and drink had been passed around the tent, he leaned closer to Ruth as he handed her a dipping bowl with oil. "I think you heard me speak with Mistress Akiva this morning." He spoke softly.

Ruth kept her focus on the barley cake in her hand. "I

did not intend to interrupt you."

"My words may have seemed odd." He took a deep breath. "I respect the work you do to provide for others. You, Maria, and the gleaners work hard. I mean you no insult in what I said to Akiva. Joshim is my dearest friend, and I fear his sister would like more from me than I am willing to provide."

"You do not want to unite with her?"

"She is a good woman, but not one I wish to have a closer relationship with. Forgive me, I have no right to speak such to you, but I could not have you think I would insult the good you do."

Ruth dipped her cake in the seasoned oil. "She is a kind woman. It is good you do not make her think more of you than she should."

Maria sat beside Ruth. "Elway fell asleep on the blanket."

***

Naomi breathed deeply as she reached the top of the hill near Zirre's shop. Almost daily walks into the town improved her strength. The beat of her heart was fast, and a smile lurked nearby. She turned. The avenue curved. Trees above the stone walls moved in a warm spring breeze. Something other than sorrow made the sight pleasing. She tightened her arms on the package she carried and went to meet Zirre.

"What do you have here?" Zirre touched a bit of fabric hanging from Naomi's bag.

Naomi tugged on the corner so more of the yellow could be seen. "Elimelech found it on one of his travels East. He had stored it in the rafters and forget when we were sent to Moab."

Zirre motioned for Naomi to follow her to the back of

the shop where light spilled through open blankets. "This is a fine weave," she declared as she spread the fabric across seed bags. "They must have access to Goldenrod flowers to get this yellow color." She peered at Naomi. "Will make a lovely dress."

Naomi nodded. "Not for me." Though sadness tinged the tone of her voice, there was a gleam. "Ruth has had little joy since Mahlon's passing. A new dress that hasn't been in dirty fields…"

Zirre slowly smiled. "I can think of one occasion where a new dress would be welcome." She ran her finger along the warp direction of the fabric. "I have a soft brown. I intended it for a bag but would make an apron."

"I don't have money. We'll bring a bag of barley for you."

"There is no need to do that."

Naomi gripped her bag. "Yes, there is."

"A small sum, perhaps." She turned her attention back to the fabric. "I will enjoy making something beautiful with this."

Chapter Tsha-esre (nineteen)

The week turned into similar rhythm as with the barley harvesting. By the fourth day, Chamishi, another row of grains dried in the garden. Through the morning, dark clouds moved from the west. One of the overseers waved at Maria and Ruth. "Blessings to you this day."

Ruth paused; wiping sweat from her brow. Maria rubbed a spot on her lower back as Elway jiggled his legs. "The Lord guide your steps."

"Seers from Bethlehem warn of storms today. Lord Boaz is sending bread and cheese to all the workers. He will not set up a meal tent today. Work as long as you may but keep watch. Return home before the storms arrive."

"Please, thank him for his kindness." Ruth took a pouch for herself and Maria and placed them in her apron.

"Another overseer will bring water." He nodded his head and walked away.

After he was gone, Maria rubbed her hands. "These stalks are tougher than the barley."

"Do you think they'll make better bricks?" Ruth pressed another sheath into her bag.

Maria shrugged. "I never knew what constituted building materials. I planned to be a wife taking care of the home. I may have wanted to work with pottery."

"Pottery? How did you learn about that?"

They continued to chat as they followed the reapers. Elway grew restless as the air stilled and humidity made drops of sweat cling to them. Workers dwindled in numbers. A large man drew close to them holding his cap in his hands. "Mistresses." He spoke as he looked at the ground.

Maria smiled. "It is good to see you, Reuben, have you been well?"

"I work. It is good. Master Daniel is leading the animals to their shelter. He said to return to your homes. The storms are close."

"Are you on your way, too?"

He nodded. "Yes, mistress. He said to go now before it rains. I go now."

"Thank you, Reuben. We will be on our way."

Sounds of the storm could be heard in the distance as they headed toward Bethlehem. Ruth swung her bag as they walked. "It's not half full. Will make going up the hill easier."

Maria chuckled. "Trust you to find our good. At least rain will clear the air." Lightning flashed across the sky followed by a long low rumble causing the earth to shake. Maria's giggle sounded more uncertain. "We'd best hurry."

Ruth adjusted the bag to get a better grip. "Our house is closer."

A second crack of thunder convinced Maria. "I think that is a wise choice."

The first large splashes of rain fell as they reached the house. A moment later, a torrent of rain clattered on the overhang and dripped down like a sheet. Ruth rubbed water from her arms as she dropped the bag against the house. Maria set her bag beside Ruth's. Another flash of lightning led to a clack of thunder. Elway screamed, beating his feet against Maria's back. The women laughed. Ruth reached around to loosen the baby.

"YHWH be praised, you made it home before the storm." Naomi greeted them in the doorway. She could barely be heard above the noise of the rain. She waved them inside.

Elway's screams did not wane.

"Here, let me," Naomi said then lifted him from Maria and held him tight against her chest. "The blanket." She held her hand out. Maria gave it to her. Naomi swaddled the baby, covering all but his face, then continued to hold him close. Cries subdued.

Maria sighed. "You are a wonder."

Naomi sat on a bench. "It is the only way I kept Chillion calm." She grinned at Ruth. "Mahlon had an easier time."

Ruth touched the head of the baby. "I'm glad he is well." More thundered rolled across the sky, but Elway didn't fuss. Ruth motioned toward Maria. "This is my friend from the fields, Maria. We've been supporting each other."

"You are welcome, my dear. I am sorry to hear of your husband passing." She glanced down at the staring boy. "You have a fine son."

"His name is Elway. I am dearly grateful for him."

Naomi blinked, but said nothing.

Ruth stood. "I can prepare a light supper, if you want to remain here."

"I will go with you. Elway is in capable hands."

Naomi rocked the baby in her arms. "Stew is in the

pot on the fire. Flatbread would be nice."

Light from the fire on the far side of the kitchen helped with the darkness of the storm. Rain poured.

Maria walked across the room. "Doesn't look like a kitchen that has been abandoned for fifteen years."

"Naomi's kin and friends have done wonders." Ruth walked to a jar with flour for making flatbread. She nodded in the direction of a ladle. "Water should be easy to get."

Rain poured down. Maria held the ladle outside the open door. Before long, Ruth kneaded dough then set a pan on the coals to cook the bread. An hour later, the three women sat at the small table on the patio listening to rain dripping from the edges of the roof as they savored the stew. Ruth dipped her bread into the thick juice.

Elway sat in a pan on the floor. his pudgy hands beat a spoon against the side. Maria sighed. "These weeks pass quickly. He'll be too big to carry before the end of the harvest."

"Then you should leave him here during the day," Naomi said.

Both Ruth and Maria looked at her. Ruth smiled. "Are you sure you want that? It's been a while since you've had a child that young."

Maria shook her head. "There are only a few more weeks before the grain harvest ends. Elway will be fine."

Naomi laughed. "I am not such an old doddered I can't care for a baby. Make your way here in the morning to leave him with me. We are not that far from your destination." She glanced at Ruth. "The two of you can walk to the fields together."

Ruth thought to object, but Naomi seemed more and

more like her old self. Perhaps having Elway to watch over would be good for her. For them both. Ruth placed her hand on Maria's arm. "He will have space to roam. We'll come back one afternoon to find him crawling."

Maria chewed her bottom lip. "Are you sure? I would not want to be a bother."

"I am pleased to have him."

***

Maria reached around a third time, then tugged on the bag of grain she carried.

Ruth rubbed her shoulder. "If we skip the meal, we can finish early and return to Naomi."

She sighed. "The meal is the best I get."

Daniel came near, leading a donkey with a water bladder across its back. "The Lord bless you." He shaded his eyes and frowned. "Is Elway ill?"

"Oh, no." Maria assured. "Naomi offered to keep him."

"You must be missing him horribly." He blushed and looked down.

Maria did not seem to notice his discomfort. "I feel strange, not having him close. Mistress Naomi thought we might work faster, but I fear I am too distracted."

Ruth shook her head. "We already have more than I imagine possible. There is no harm in a slower day."

Daniel handed them water. "Lord Boaz will make certain you have what you need."

Ruth assumed he meant regarding gathered wheat, but when they ducked into the lunch tent, away from the glaring sun heating the afternoon, Naomi called to them. With a cry of delight, Maria rushed around Ruth and gathered her son close. Ruth joined Naomi at the table. "This is a welcome surprise. Did you walk all this way with the baby?"

Naomi tapped Ruth's knee. "I could have." She smiled at Daniel, whose attention was on Maria and Elway. "This good man brought a wagon to the house and offered us lunch."

"I may not have children, but I understand the joy they give." Boaz sat beside Naomi. "Greetings, cousin."

"May YHWH's hand be ever upon you." Naomi returned a salutation. "This allows me a proper thank you. For meeting with Judge Ehud and settling the matter with Hador."

Boaz glanced at Ruth. "Did you tell her about his visit afterwards?"

"She said you kept her from hitting him with the garden tool." Nomi grinned.

"Serena asks if you would sit with her at the reading of the Word on Sabbath and then join us for a meal at our house."

Ruth sat straight. "You provide so much during the week. We cannot."

"It is to our honor," Boaz said with a smile.

Naomi patted Ruth's hand. "They are family. We will return the favor someday soon."

***

Rays of sun spilled across the hills, color of twilight crossing the sky. Insects chirped and the distinct call of a hawk on the hunt sounded. Ruth closed her eyes and breathed. Her arms ached and the thought of having to bend made her cringe, but the fruit of her labor spread through covered areas around the house. "YHWH." His name sounded strange in her voice, but something within yearned to speak. What would the priest read on the morrow? Would it be rules and sacrifices she struggled to understand? Would it be stories of the first family, or how the great sea spread when Father Moses held his rod over the waters? Stories kept her attention more. A yawn made her close her eyes. She breathed the night air and headed to bed.

Eagerness drew her awake as jays squawked from trees along the road. Sabbath. A day of rest and a day of worship. Not having to go to the fields brought a sigh of contentment. They were gathering in Bethlehem to hear the priest read the words of YHWH. Ruth pulled her kethoneth tunic over her head and tied beige cords at her waist. She draped her matching scarf to cover her hair.

Naomi offered a cup of tea and bowl of warmed oats drizzled with honey. The women enjoyed their break of fast then walked into Bethlehem. With blue sky and warm sun overhead, they sat beneath olive trees. Talia plopped down beside them. Serena followed at a more-sedate pace. She spread a blanket for them and offered Naomi the use of a small pillow as she leaned on the tree trunk.

The priest read stories from a book called Genesis. Ruth leaned forward. She'd heard these before. How could anything, or anyone good survive in a world where everyone was bad? Her thoughts drifted to Father. Was he bad the way people in the time of Noah were bad? Or had he not known how to raise a daughter? She shook herself and refocused her attention on the priest. She looked forward to the meal with Serena and then a quiet evening. Tomorrow would be another day for harvesting.

Fourth Week of the Month of Iyar
Chapter Eshrim (twenty)

Six weeks in Bethlehem. Ruth smiled at Maria. Adjusting to not having her son with her on the fields, Maria pushed two handfuls of wheat into her bag. They stopped suddenly. "Did you hear that?" Maria asked as she gazed toward the west.

A cry had risen. As they watched, several reapers moved to a shaded area. A moment later, a large man ran in their direction. It didn't take long to recognize Reuben. When he was close enough, his face seemed pale and he breathed hard.

Ruth pressed her hand against her chest. "What has happened?"

"One of the overseers has been wounded. I must fetch Lord Boaz." The young worker cried as he ran past. Ruth and Maria kept their eyes on the growing crowd in the distance. If the wound were minor, would they still be there? Ruth swallowed. "We should go, offer aid as we may."

Maria nodded. They dropped the bags, lifted their skirts, and ran.

"Who is it?" Maria gasped as they drew close.

"I didn't mean to. It was an accident. He startled me."

"Accident or no, you best head to one of the sanctuary

cities."

"How am I to do that?"

Men looked at each other. "How far is Shechem? Or Hebron for that matter?"

Another man waved a hand. "What of Kadesh, mightn't that be closer?"

"Is he dead?" Maria asked as she placed her hand on the arm of an elder, then dropped it when he turned to look at her.

"His wound is likely mortal."

Ruth felt her heart drop as the man moved and the wounded overseer could be seen. "Maria, it's Daniel."

With a cry, the other woman fell to her knees beside him. He showed no response. Blood soaked the front of his shirt.

Ruth unhooked the apron at her waist. "Try to stop the blood." She tossed it to Maria. Ruth searched the gawkers. "Fetch water, and more linens." She noticed a servant who had assisted with lunch. "Are there any of the plantains left? The pulp and rind could be useful."

The servant seemed pale. He nodded and ran. Someone bumped into Ruth, splashing water on her feet. "Make room," she pushed others away so she could sit beside Maria.

"You can't save him," someone muttered.

They both ignored him. Ruth wet part of the apron. "Wash the wound. We have to get the fibers from his shirt out of it." A jagged slash ran from his side across his chest.

Maria wiped at her eyes. "He must have startled him as he was cutting the wheat."

Ruth swallowed. "Hand me the apron." She glanced at the men hovering nearby. "More water. Find another bucket." She dipped the apron in the water. Red swirled around her hands. "Here," she wrung the cloth. "Clean what you can."

"Is he dead? Why do you bother?"

Ruth wanted to tell them to go away, but the rise and fall of Daniel's chest meant he lived and needed their help. Maria handed the apron back. She cleaned what she could again. Ruth glared at the men still there. "We'll need a large blanket to move him carefully."

"Move him where? He has no one."

"Move him to my house," Maria said as she reached for more water. "I will care for him."

They left, disapproval on their faces.

"I hope they bring something to move him with."

The servant returned breathing hard. He carried a long flat woven tray. "I found what I could."

"May the hand of YHWH bless you." Ruth took the tray. She mashed plantains into a doughy mess. "Does there look to be any cloth in the wound? It could bring sickness."

Maria sobbed. "I don't know. I can't tell. Do we have fresh water?"

"Here, mistress." A boy breathing hard from a run to the stream at the bottom of the fields set a second pail beside Maria.

Blood still seeped from the wound, but they managed to wash most of his skin clear. "Use it like a poultice," Ruth said as she took Maria's hand and filled it with a plop of plantain. "This should help slow bleeding."

A horse could be heard crossing the field. Ruth shaded her eyes to see the tall shape clearer. She stood as she recognized the rider. "Lord Boaz."

Boaz slid from the horse and hurried to them.

"Someone said a man's been killed. What are you doing?"

"He's not dead, but gravely wounded." She leaned over the basket and picked out a few large leaves. "Here." She handed them to Maria. "Cover the pulp, and then we will need help to bind him."

"Daniel," Boaz cried out. He went to the other side and knelt by him. "He's not dead?" He looked to Ruth.

"He is still breathing. They must carry him as gently as possible."

"Who will care for him?"

"I will." Maria spoke firmly.

"Where is the man responsible?"

Ruth searched the few remaining workers. "I don't see him."

"Here is a blanket that should be strong enough to carry him." A reaper hurried to Ruth with the blanket tossed over his arm.

"Lay it flat on the ground over here." Ruth stood as she indicated the space beside them. She turned to Boaz. "If you hold him under his arms and two men lift his feet, Maria and I can wrap and secure the wound. Then place him on the blanket." She peered at the two men who moved closer to Daniel's feet. "His life may depend on you. Be careful."

Ruth tried not to wince as she spied their struggle. She and Maria used a long skull wrap to bind Daniel's chest. When they finally placed him on the blanket, there was not much more blood. He moaned but didn't open his eyes.

Maria stood next to Ruth. "Our bags are still in the field."

"I will get them and finish what I can. Later tonight

I'll bring Elway and check Daniel's wound."

"Thank you, dear friend." She squeezed her hand.

"Be as steady as you can," Ruth told the servants who were prepared to carry Daniel from the field.

"YHWH guide your steps," Boaz added. The two of them watched the slow procession, then Boaz gazed down on Ruth. "How may I help?"

"There is not much more to do. I have seen such wounds survive, but I've also seen them die."

"What help do you need? Where are the bags?"

"Over there." Ruth pointed eastward.

"Lead the way."

"You shouldn't…"

"It will help the others return to work." He slowed his walk so Ruth didn't feel rushed.

"Will the horse be okay?"

"He'll follow me and enjoy some oats along the way."

When they were back where Ruth had started, Ruth leaned over for the larger sack.

"Allow me," Boaz managed to heft one bag over his shoulder and hold the second one open to fill.

Ruth grinned, then they got to work. "Yesterday's reading spoke of working the land by sweat." She used a corner of her apron to wipe her forehead. "Is all this because of what happened in the beginning?"

"I've not thought of it as such," Boaz pushed the plants so Ruth could fit another sheave. "Summer heat brings out the fruits and prepares the olives. They are worth our toil now."

"Do you think they made it to Maria's house?"

Boaz turned to look. "I asked her to send Reuben. He may be a simple man, but he is trustworthy and steadfast."

***

With Boaz' assistance, she finished gleaning what could fit in the bags. Boaz carried them to the processing barn. "You do not need to wait. I'll bring them. Will you head directly to Mistress Maria's?"

She shook her head. "I told her I would get Elway and then go."

"Wait for me. I will bring a wagon. We may need to gather supplies."

"I pray your friend heals."

Boaz faced her and sighed. "I know his life is in the hands of YHWH, but still I fear for him."

"He is young, and I think he has something to live for."

"I will meet you at Naomi's."

Ruth hurried across the fields and up into Bethlehem. Naomi sat on a bench in the garden, watching Elway dig into a soft mound of dirt mixed with sand. Ruth didn't mind the grubby hands reaching for her and she picked him up.

"You are home early," Naomi said with a smile and then her eyes widened. "Is that blood?"

Ruth looked down. Rust-colored stains marred her tunic. "There was an accident in the fields. Do you remember the overseer Daniel? He was cut badly with a blade."

Naomi stood. "The young man who helped repair our house?"

"Yes. Lord Boaz is bringing a wagon and we will take Elway home. I will make a fresh poultice to put on the wound. More bandages." She held Elway close, kissing his cheek. "Lord Boaz said Daniel's life is in the hands of YHWH, but how do you ask for healing if there is no statue to offer sacrifice to?"

Naomi stepped close and took Ruth's free hand. "We pray. Lord most high, save your servant Daniel. Give us the wisdom to address his needs."

By the time Boaz arrived, the women had a basket of bandages, food, and some men's clothes. Ruth tapped the package she kept close to her sleeping pad. A few items belonging to Mahlon. Of course, Maria may already have items belonging to her husband, but Ruth felt the time had come to completely release what had been.

The ride to Maria's was quiet. The small space built among a row of houses had a linen curtain covering the main entrance. Different sized clay pots sat in the opening. Boaz went first and took the basket from Ruth. Daniel lay on the far side of the room, past a small hearth. The large opening on the other side of him led to the outdoor cooking area and a space for Elway to crawl around. Maria came through with a small bowl of water.

She greeted the others. "They made him as comfortable as possible." She moved around Daniel and handed the bowl to Boaz. "Do you want to give him a bit to drink? Lift his head gently. I'll help Ruth empty the basket."

Boaz did as directed. Ruth noticed Daniel open his eyes and offer a wan smile to his friend. Ruth gave Maria a handful of cloths to dress the wound. "How is he?"

"They moved him with care. There was a little blood. I washed it away already. He woke but doesn't seem capable of talking. He must be in great pain."

Ruth picked up a box. "Naomi and I brought this from Moab. Mix a little with water and let him drink it. It should ease the pain and help him to sleep."

Maria smelled the powder and made a face. "What is

it?"

Ruth shrugged. "Healers use ground bark from a willow tree, and something used in the temples. There is only enough to aid sleep, nothing harmful should come of it. "

"Is there still water in the bowl?" Maria looked at Boaz. At his nod, she motioned for him to bring it to them.

"Use a spoon," Ruth suggested. They added the powder to the water, mixed, then had Boaz return to Daniel. "Try to have him drink as much as possible."

Elway crawled to his mother and sat with a whimper. Maria lifted him in her arms. "Did you see that? He'll be walking in no time." She pondered the doorway. "I'll have to find something to block the entrance."

They sat and talked for an hour. Boaz joined them as Daniel slipped into a restful sleep. Maria bounced Elway on her lap. "Does Daniel have family who should know where he is?"

"I found him in Jerusalem and convinced him to come work for me. He has no family I know of."

Ruth noticed Maria's glance across the room. Perhaps he did have family.

"Stay with him these next few days," Boaz told Maria as he and Ruth prepared to leave. "I will provide for you both."

"I will come in the morning," Ruth told her. "We should change the poultice and make sure the wound looks clean. I'll take Elway to Naomi."

"You don't have to; I will be here."

"She enjoys having him."

There was nothing more to contend. Boaz lit a lantern that hung in the room. With a prayer for Daniel's healing, he and Ruth took their leave. Ruth tried to head for home on her own, but Boaz insisted on taking her by wagon.

"What will happen to the man who stabbed Daniel?" she asked as the horse kept a slow pace through Bethlehem.

"Witnesses say he has already gone to a sanctuary city. It is not necessary, but there is no way to call him back."

"What do you mean?"

"Sanctuary cities were ordained by YHWH to prevent revenge at the hands of family when someone has been killed. As long as a person remains within the city, no one may harm him. The Levites would mediate if Daniel had family that demanded reparation."

"A strange practice."

"Is it? People tend to act brashly in the heat of the moment. The mediator has not those passions."

They arrived at Naomi's house. Ruth stood. "That is something to think upon."

Boaz nodded. "I will help you tomorrow."

"There is no need."

He smiled. "And yet, I still will. The Lord bless you for your help today. You may have saved Daniel's life."

Ruth glanced down as heat flushed her cheeks. "We were all needed. Good night." She took a step back, watching him against the deepening twilight. He nodded, and she smiled gently. It wasn't until he had gone that she pressed her hand against the flutterings inside her belly.

132

Chapter Eshrim ve Ehad (twenty-one)

By Chamishi, the fifth day of the week, Ruth was pleased to see Daniel raised up, leaning against cushions. The wound remained clear, and they wrapped without the use of a poultice. Ruth stood out front with Maria while Lord Boaz talked with Daniel. They paused their conversation as an older woman glared while passing Maria.

Ruth frowned. "What is that about?"

Maria sighed. "They are against my bringing Daniel home to convalesce." Her frown deepened. "Some think it would have been better for him to die."

"What a horrible notion," Ruth gasped.

Maria breathed. "I refuse to be intimidated. You understand his need to be here."

"As do Lord Boaz and Naomi. Others as well. They've brought you food and supplies."

"Most have come from Lord Boaz. But yes, Zirre has brought bread and smoked meats. Batya, too."

Ruth grasped her hand. "All your friends who care for you know you would never act dishonorably."

"I am glad you came with Naomi to Bethlehem."

"As am I." Ruth glanced back at the house. "Let Lord Boaz know I walked home. I promised Naomi I'd help with our evening meal."

Ruth appreciated the breeze on the warm afternoon. They had only needed half a day to glean. The wheat harvest was soon over. In the following week, men would celebrate the harvests, making use of the outdoor threshing floors and the barn.

The sun dropped toward the horizon when Ruth turned the corner toward home. Her steps slowed when she noticed Hador leaned against the rock wall. She could not really see a smile through his beard. His eyes made her stiffen her back.

"Your mother-in-law is a difficult woman to approach."

"She knows who her friends are. What did you do?"

"I've tried to help." He stepped away from the wall. "The field and house have not been claimed by either redeemer." He moved closer. "You have not been claimed."

Ruth tightened her grip on the basket. "I am not property to be claimed. I am a widow. My husband was an honorable man. As such, I will be treated with honor."

"But was he?" He frowned. "Mahlon lived half his life in Moab. He died there. What honor is due him in Bethlehem? I am a good man. Give yourself to me and I will restore Mahlon and his family."

"You may think yourself good, but you are not honorable. An honorable man would not try to steal what is not his, nor would he force his attention on those who have already denied him."

"Your pretty words won't mean much if you are despoiled. What peace would you have in Bethlehem if you became known as a harlot?"

"You have said quite enough." Boaz' voice came from behind her.

Ruth kept her shoulders stiff as she glared at Hador. "No one would believe your lies. Your pride and disregard for others will be your undoing."

"This stops now." Boaz jumped from his horse. "Any further harassment of Mistress Naomi or Ruth, and both I and Athor will approach the city council to have you thrown out of Bethlehem."

"I don't see why your claim should have any more merit than my own. Look at your parents." Hador scowled.

Boaz' face darkened, but Ruth laughed. "You call into question the likes of Lord Boaz? I am a foreigner and even I can see he is a man of honor and integrity."

Hador's ears darkened to red. His mouth opened.

"Before you say anything further, consider who is here." Boaz motioned to a group drawing near along the road from the other direction. Ruth recognized Zirre and Joshim.

"Maligning a leader of our tribe would hurt your ability to do business in Bethlehem," Zirre said as she stood frowning, arms crossed.

Ruth smiled at Naomi's friend. Silver hair and wrinkles did not detract from the force of her statement.

With short, angry breaths, Hador peered at the house and the edge of the field visible below. "None of you need…"

"It is not yours. Release this evil from your heart." Zirre stepped closer.

Hador raised his hand to strike her, but Boaz grabbed his arm and the younger man could not pull away. "You go too far. Be gone."

Overpowered and outnumbered, he did as he was told, but Ruth felt cold at the sting of anger in his eyes. "He is wicked like my father."

Zirre put an arm around her shoulders. "He is capable of better but makes poor choices. Come, let us visit with Naomi."

Ruth turned to Boaz. "Thank you for your help. Are the others well?"

He nodded. "Daniel fares better than expected. He has good help. I wanted to be sure you arrived home safely."

She chuckled. "Everything was fine until I got here."

"Come, we should help prepare the evening meal." Zirre pulled her away.

***

Once they were inside, Zirre removed her sandals. "Nasty business. I hope Hador learns his lesson before he comes to harm."

"What nasty business?" Naomi asked, wiping her hands as she crossed the room toward them.

"Hador making a fool of himself," Zirre explained as she opened the package she carried. "Joshim and Lord Boaz set him straight."

Ruth looked around. "Was Joshim with you? Where did he go?"

"We met on the way. He wanted to talk with Boaz. Here, I finished." She drew out a tunic made from the yellow fabric. The cut was simple, but an intricate design had been embroidered on the neck and sleeves.

"Beautiful," Ruth exclaimed. She touched gently. "It's the fabric we found in the barn." She smiled at Naomi. "This shade will look lovely on you."

Naomi grinned. "Thank you, daughter, but it is not for me."

Her eyes widened as she realized they meant her to have it. "But what would I do with a fine dress?"

Naomi's smile remained mysterious. "We'll put it away for now, but when the time comes, you will know."

She hugged Naomi, and the feel of being wrapped in her mother's arms brought tears to her eyes. "Thank you." Her voice sounded scruffy.

Naomi kissed her temple. "Thank you."

With a laugh, she hugged Zirre as well. They held the dress against her to see how it would look, but Ruth was reluctant to try it on. "Not yet. Not until there could be a real purpose for it."

***

Ruth dreamt of her father. The layer of hay beneath her mat could not cushion her from memory of his fists, nor block her from the acrid tone of his voice. She jerked awake with a gasp. Her heart pounded as she gazed across the upper hall. Nights were not hot enough to move outdoors, but stars of the night sky could be seen through the open doorway. A wisp of cloud curled and twisted along its way, driven by an unseen breeze. Ruth blinked. There seemed to be more of the clouds spreading into the night. As her fears calmed, she realized there really was an acrid smell in the air. She got to her feet and ran to the balcony. A small fire licked at the olive tree growing in the garden. Ruth ran back into the house. "Mother, Mother Naomi," she shook her gently, but her voice conveyed urgency.

Naomi sat up. "What is it, my child?"

"There is a fire in the garden. I saw from the balcony, so I don't know how bad. I'm going to try to put it out."

"I must help." She pushed herself to her feet.

"What about going to a neighbor for help?"

"Yes," Naomi rubbed her face. "Yes, of course. That would make sense."

Ruth headed for the stairs. "Can you see to get down?"

"I'll be fine. Put your sandals on. Try to protect yourself. Should the fire grow too large, step away. Don't let yourself be harmed."

Ruth looked back at Naomi, nodded, and then hurried down the stairs. She grabbed a pitcher of water and an old tunic lying in a pile to be mended. Though there was plenty of smoke, the fire did not seem to be devouring the tree. Ruth soaked the tunic with water and slapped it against the flames. Fire moved, but moments later it was back again. She struck a second time. There was the sound of Naomi leaving, but Ruth did not make time to look. She stomped an ember that strayed from the tree onto the ground. Her efforts kept the fire contained, but she could not make it go out.

Others were running toward the house as she hurried back with another pitcher of water. They brought buckets and bowls with them, drawing water from the animal's trough.

When the sun kissed the horizon, the garden had been trampled, and the thick bark of the olive tree turned black.

"You will share what we have. Once everyone has a chance to rest, we will replant your garden. In a month we won't be able to tell fire had been here."

A thin, tall neighbor scowled. "There were no storms in the night. No lightning."

Zirre wrapped a blanket around Naomi's shoulders. "We all know who did this."

Joshim held an axe. "If you are referring to Hador, he was seen fleeing Bethlehem while it was still dark. He likely started this, but he will not be allowed to return."

Naomi nodded. "Thank you for your help."

He grinned. "We have festival days ahead of us. Better for him to be gone so we may enjoy the fruits of our labor."

Naomi leaned against her friend. "YHWH has blessed us, not just here, today, but throughout the harvest."

Akiva arrived with a large basket. "You have endured a hard night. Here you may take your fast and then rest." She walked to Ruth. "I sent word to your friend, Maria. The baby will remain with them today."

"But Daniel—"

"He is content." She smiled. "I believe they both are. Perhaps after the festival days, we will have something else to celebrate."

Sometime later, though still early, Naomi and Ruth settled with a cup of tea. Everyone had gone. "I am thankful he did not have skill for starting fires." Naomi sighed.

Ruth leaned her head against Naomi's shoulder. "No one is hurt. Little damage. Hador is gone."

"Yes, although I hope he learns peace. Life is hard without it."

"Do you forgive him?"

Naomi took her hand. "Yes, I forgive him. I do not understand his struggles, so I pray he will find a better way."

"Should I forgive my father? How would I even do that?"

Naomi thought for a moment. "Your father was a hard man. I do not know what led him to be that way. Do you?"

"No."

"It had to be pain he never released. Try to let go of your hurt."

"I had a dream last night. I woke because of it."

"That is worth forgiveness." Naomi yawned. "It seems wicked to think about sleeping during the day, but I feel exhausted."

"Sleep for a little while, then later we can take these clothes to wash."

Naomi laughed. "And wash us."

***

Ruth didn't mind sitting beneath a tree listening to the Sabbath reading. Her arms ached and a burn near her wrist hurt. Instead of reading from scrolls, the priest recited the battle of Jericho. She glanced at Serena. Her mother did all that? She'd heard stories, of course, but it seemed different coming from the priest. She hadn't done anything so brave. Mahlon didn't fight for Israel, nor did she think to betray Moab to help Israel. Not that Israel had been intent on destroying Moab, merely gaining freedom.

Naomi pulled her close after they stood at the end of the reading. "Do not concern yourself with these things."

"I said nothing," Ruth protested.

Naomi laughed. "Daughter, your expressions give you away. Your story is different from Mother Rahab."

Ruth shook her head. "I have no story."

Naomi looked across the square. "It is still being written."

First Week of the Month of Sivan
Chapter Eshrim ve Shtain (twenty-two)

Naomi stood in the doorway watching Ruth curled in a chair staring across the garden. Green shoots showed through scorched earth. Kittens chased each other through wilting remnants. There was still life in the garden, the fire had not destroyed everything. She focused on Ruth. The love that welled within for the young woman overcame any lingering wisps of sorrow for her own loses. The plan forging in her mind brought a smile to her face. She stepped over to Ruth and grasped the young woman's hand with both of hers.

Ruth looked up and made to stand, but Naomi shook her head. "My daughter, should I not seek rest for you, that it may be well with you?"

"I don't mind the work to be done."

"Of course not. You are a daughter of honor. I speak of our relatives, the owner of the fields where you harvested."

"Lord Boaz?" Ruth asked as her cheeks reddened.

Naomi smiled and nodded. "He is winnowing barley at the threshing floor tonight."

"That is not a place for gleaners."

"No. I have other business in mind. Wash and anoint yourself. Put on your cloak and go down to the threshing floor. Do not let anyone see you, not even Lord Boaz. There will be drinking and eating, you know how these things go. Wait until everyone is settled. Watch for where Lord Boaz lies down. When you are ready, go and uncover his feet and lie down. He will tell you what to do."

Ruth didn't take time to consider. She squeezed Naomi's hand and nodded. "All that you say I will do."

"You trust Lord Boaz?"

Ruth paused, but her gray eyes gleamed. "I do trust him."

* * *

Ruth slipped bangles over her thin wrists. A shake of her hand made the thin bands of metal hit against each other. If the butterflies in her stomach could make noise-- She pulled the bangles off. "Too much noise might attract attention." Too bad the butterflies were not as easy to get rid of.

What if he didn't offer her protection? What if he grew to resent her, a foreigner? Would he become like her father with a painful fist? Her hands started to shake, and tears pooled in her eyes. This wasn't a good idea. She would have to tell Naomi.

Something glittered through the open window. Ruth turned. The setting sun crept from beneath the edge of a cloud, sending rays like fingers stretching across the sky. Golden light splashed on mounds of drying barley and wheat. Thoughts of Boaz' kindness came to mind. Guiding her across Bethlehem to find the best merchants for the extra grains. Helping her when Maria went to save Daniel's life. Sending workers to prepare Naomi's home for upcoming summer storms and winter cold. Memory of his virtue calmed her fear. In the beauty of the moment, her mind thought on the One who had led her to this time and place.

"I do not understand you as I should," her voice sounded small as she spoke into the waning afternoon. "I do not feel worthy of your name. You have led Mother Naomi and me to Bethlehem. You have guided and blessed. If our plan is noble and right, then fulfill what has been growing in my heart."

There was no carved image of wood or stone, only the wind and gleam of light falling from the clouds. *In the Beginning.* The words spoken by the priest came to mind. This beginning would be a good thing.

***

Darkness had fallen by the time she left their home. Naomi remained in a window illuminated by a nearby candle. The soft glow of candlelight eased the harsh lines on her face. The woman looking out appeared much like her old self. Ruth waved, then wrapped the cloak around her like a shadow. Crickets sang. The gurgling croak of frogs sounded as she passed beneath the gate. No one seemed to notice her. The first quarter moon hung in the west. Once she made it down the hill, she took a path to her right into the fields. Before she reached the first short fence of rock, laughter from the threshing floor sounded around her. She moved towards a narrow stretch of trees.

The cloak kept her from shivering as the late spring evening settled around them.

Heavy laughter and shouts accompanied large fires. Ruth dozed with her back against a tree. When she woke, stars twinkled overhead. The quarter moon kissed the western horizon. Light from the fires had dimmed. Voices were more muted.

Boaz spoke to someone. She recognized the timbre of his voice though she could not understand what he said. She peaked, eager to watch where he settled. Servants and lead reapers settled deep within the threshing floor. Boaz, with his richly colored cloak lined with purple frills settled nearer the edge, a place where he could stare out into the starlit sky. She smiled. Though he was older, his shoulders were wide, and he stood taller than most. He lay beneath the arch keystone etched with a crossing scythe and wheat frond.

Murmurs and shuffling dimmed then quieted. Flames darkened though they did not go out. A few men sat and chatted a bit longer. Ruth kept her eye on the section where Boaz lay. With a chorus of crickets and a lone cry in the field far away surrounding her, Ruth finally stepped from the safety of the trees. Getting caught here, at this time, people would think horrible things about her, especially as a foreign-born woman. She moved on despite her fears.

Boaz had set himself a little apart from the others. He lay on his back, one arm curled above his head. Even in the dark of night, his features were recognizable. She stood for a moment admiring. Even in sleep his mouth opened, and a grunt made her grin. Mahlon snored horribly. Boaz did not sound near as harsh. With a breath of courage, Ruth threw back the cover from Boaz' feet. The slight chill in the air should garner his attention at some point. She lay at his feet, a willing servant, awaiting his redemption.

Night had deepened when Ruth felt Boaz move. His foot struck her arm, and she gasped.

"Who are you?" Boaz hissed.

Ruth sat up, drawing her cloak close around her.

Though her hands shook, she spoke clearly. "I am your servant, Ruth."

Boaz raised up on his elbow to peer at her in the darkness. "Why are you here?"

"Spread your wings over your servant, for you are a redeemer."

"May you be blessed by YHWH." He sat; legs crossed. He tossed the blanket to cover his feet as well as Ruth's. "Your kindness at the last is greater than the first you paid to Naomi. You have not gone after young men, though rich and poor would have taken you in."

Ruth felt heat burning her cheeks and hoped he couldn't tell. She lowered her face. "I have not desired to go to any other."

"Do not fear. Everyone knows you are a worthy woman. It is true, I am a redeemer. But there is a redeemer closer than I. Remain tonight. In the morning, I will approach him. If he will redeem you, good; let him do it. If he is not willing to redeem you, then as the Lord lives, I will redeem you. Stay until morning."

Ruth rubbed her hand against the scratch of his coarse covering. "I should return to Naomi."

"It is not safe in the night. Rest here. I will help you leave at first light."

An unseen animal called through the dark. Ruth returned to her place at Boaz' feet. A layer of hay softened the hard ground. The addition of Boaz' cloak kept the chill away. She closed her eyes. Rather than remaining awake in fear, a sense of protection welled through the butterflies that still fluttered inside her. She slept, until Boaz moving woke her.

Although stars glimmered to the west, dawn lit the eastern sky, providing light to see. Ruth sat, and felt her hair fall around her shoulders. Boaz' hair stuck out, and bits of the hay were tangled in his beard. For a moment, she feared looking in his eyes, feared his decision in the dark would be different now.

"Good morning," he greeted quietly.

When she lifted her face, the warmth in his glance left her with no doubts. "Blessings upon you this day."

He grinned. "Great blessings indeed. I think now is time for you to return home. I don't want any to know a woman came to the threshing floor last night." He pushed to his feet, then offered his hand to help her stand.

Ruth flicked the side of her dress and swiped at some stray bits of hay and dirt.

"Bring your garment and hold it out." He led her toward the exit where several barrels of barley remained.

Ruth lifted part of her cloak and held it in her arms like a bag.

Boaz dipped a large cup into the barley, then poured it into her cloak. "You must not return empty-handed to your mother-in-law." He poured another five measures.

Ruth tightened her grip with a giggle. "Much more, I won't be able to carry it myself." She smiled. "Thank you for your generosity."

He lifted his hand to touch her cheek but did not. "I will visit Naomi as soon as I may." Something rustled in the dimness of the threshing floor. "Now go, YHWH be with you."

Ruth returned to Bethlehem, though she couldn't be sure her feet ever touched the paths.

Chapter Eshrim ve Shalosh (twenty-three)

Naomi stood in the doorway as Ruth crossed to the house. "Well, my dear. How did you fare?"

Ruth's laugh turned into a hiccup. "He gave me barley, six measures of it."

"Over there," Naomi pointed to the shed across the courtyard. "Zirre picked up a bag yesterday so there is room in the trough."

Ruth and Naomi managed to get most of the barley in the trough. With her arms freed, Ruth hugged Naomi. "He will redeem me." She pulled away. "At least, he said there is someone closer. Who could he mean?"

"Must be Elimelech's nephew, his brother's son. You have met him." Naomi linked arms with Ruth to walk back to the house. "Athor."

"The young man? Do you think he would want to marry me?"

"Would you be opposed to him? He has the first right."

Ruth was quiet. Athor had been nice enough, but marriage to him was not on her mind. Or her heart.

Naomi patted her hand. "Wait until you learn how the matter turns out, my daughter. Boaz will not rest until he settles the matter today."

***

"Tuvya, I am pleased to greet you this morning. Have you seen Yosef?"

"Well met, Lord Boaz." The larger man shook Boaz's hand, then waved at someone further away. "Here is my red-headed friend." He laughed as Yosef drew closer.

"A fine day, though I think it will rain this afternoon." The other man nodded in greeting. Red hair had covered his head at one time, now all that remained was a ring.

Boaz shook Josef's hand. "What other men will be in the gate this morning?"

Tuvya raised a white-crested brown. "Have you business with the elders?"

"I do, yes." Boaz recognized Athor leading a pack animal through the gate. "Cousin," he called. "Join me for a moment. I have business to attend with you."

"Lord Boaz," Athor lifted his hand in greeting as he led the donkey to rocks set along the path leading through the gate. "You are usually in the fields by now."

"I have come on a family matter."

Tuvya placed a hand on Boaz' shoulder to stay his greeting. After eight more elders took seats among them, Tuvya motioned for Boaz and Athor to sit. "It is a warm morning, and I am sure you have much to do with the harvest. Our next feast draws near."

"Thank you, Tuvya." Boaz turned to Athor. "We have family business to discuss."

Author settled in his seat. "Is it necessary now?"

"Our relative, Elimelech, has died, along with his sons. There are fields and properties with which to content. If we do not, someone else may. That would not benefit the widows."

"I am the nearer kin," Athor toyed with a pouch. "The field would be useful. With its profits, I could set up my own home sooner."

"It is a well-situated field. I believe both barley and wheat have grown successful."

"A good bit of business," Yosef said as the other elders tapped their legs.

Boaz halted them with a look. "Before we finalize our business, there is the matter of redeeming Naomi for the sake of her sons." Boaz directed his gaze at Athor. "To have the field, you must marry the Moabitess. You must marry Ruth and redeem the line of Elimelech."

Athor clutched his pouch, face becoming pale. "Marry Ruth? I can't. I mean, she's a good woman. I'm not sure Naomi would have made it without her." His ears reddened. "I have plans to marry. I already approached her father."

Boaz schooled his features to not show his pleasure. "You will not marry Ruth to raise offspring to Mahlon?"

"No, of course not." Athor stood, releasing the donkey to unlace his shoe. He held it toward Boaz. "I renounce my claim. I am not the redeemer who is needed."

Boaz accepted Athor's sandal. "It is well, cousin. I wish you blessing in your future." He faced the elders. "You are witnesses this day."

"Here, here," the elder's acknowledged Athor's release.

Tuvya stroked his beard as they watched Athor's hasty retreat. "Athor's choice for a bride will have a good life." He peered at Boaz. "What of Elimelech's family? Without a redeemer, they are at risk."

"I will redeem. I have the second claim."

"You?" Tavya chuckled. Others wagged their heads. "You have never wanted to marry. A great disappointment it has been to many fathers and daughters."

Boaz placed Athor's sandal in the pocket of his coat. "It is my right, and my duty. It is also what I desire. Naomi and Ruth remain in my protection. I will have the field and house. By the grace of YHWH, I will raise up offspring to perpetuate the name of Elimelech, Mahlon, and Chillion, that they may not be cut off from the land of our fathers."

"You don't mind joining your life with a foreigner? Josef questioned.

"You forget my mother," Boaz grinned at the elders. He wasn't far from their ages, but perhaps time remained for his own family. "May YHWH bless your steps. Thank you for your time." Boaz stood.

Tuvya and the other men stood as well. "We are witnesses. May the Lord make the woman coming into your house like Rachel and Leah, who built up the house of Israel. May you act worthy in Ephrathah and be renowned in Bethlehem. May your house be like the house of Perez, whom Tamar bore to Judah, because of the offspring that the Lord will give you by this young woman."

He shook hands with them then followed the path down from Bethlehem into the fields.

Chapter Eshrim ve Arba (twenty-four)

"I should have gone to work in the field," Ruth peeked through the window toward the outer fields, then paced back to the kitchen area.

Sounds of a horse could be heard in the lane. Ruth turned to Naomi. "You look."

"He will need to speak with us both. We should sit in the garden." Naomi looped her arm with Ruth's and led her through the kitchen.

Once seated, Ruth clenched her hands in her lap. Hid them beneath her apron. Pulled them out again. One of the kittens tumbled over a rock. She reached down and picked her up. The small paws played with her fingers.

"Thought I might find you here," Boaz said as he stood in the arched opening with the top of his head brushing the stone. He pulled a shoe from his pocket, set it on the bench beside Naomi, and sat beneath the olive tree. "I met with the elders in the gate this morning. Athor joined us. The sandal is his. He has released himself from any responsibility regarding your well-being, Mother Naomi. He has renounced his position as a redeemer."

"What of yourself?"

Boaz smiled, his dark eyes glittering. "I offer myself as a redeemer. I will take over the field. My men will watch the house and take care of any repairs." He looked at Ruth. "I offer you marriage. The protection of my name, and an opportunity to raise up children to Mahlon, to carry on the line of Elimelech."

Naomi stood. "You honor us, dear cousin. I will leave you to speak with Ruth." She took the kitten, squeezing Ruth's hand. "You have my blessing, but the choice remains with you."

Ruth felt her heart thumping. Boaz watched Naomi leave, and then he looked at her.

"Your actions last night led me to believe, to hope."

"I chose Mahlon because I felt safe with him. Safer than I ever felt with my father. You are different."

"I'm not safe?"

"With you, I feel cherished. Honored."

"Loved?"

His words brought a smile. "Yes, loved. You don't mind I am not a daughter of Israel?"

He laughed. "I am not fully a son of Israel, but I have never been made to feel less."

"We must not leave Naomi alone."

"Never. She will join us at our home. Will you marry me?" He stood, holding his hand toward her.

Ruth placed her hand in his and let him pull her from her seat. They were closer than they'd ever been.

"Yes."

At her confirmation, he leaned down and kissed her. Ruth felt the promise of their life together grow in her heart. Naomi did not leave them long.

Epilogue

"Another barley harvest begins, my love." Boaz wrapped his arms around Ruth as she stood in the window of their bedroom, looking out over the fields.

"Am I wrong to be thankful I have no need to glean this year?" She leaned against him as he laid his hand on her large belly.

"You are still working."

She laughed. "Is Daniel able to work in the fields?"

"I have made him overseer. The wound keeps him from full use of his arm, but he is a smart man."

"He and Maria seem able to tend the field at Elimelech's house. Thank you for providing the house to them. Elway will have another brother or sister by the summer harvest."

He kissed her, caressing her neck. "Naomi says we don't have long to wait."

"I am almost as excited as she." Ruth closed her eyes as she felt the child shift within.

Boaz chuckled. "He will be a strong lad."

"A son would be a blessing. The line of Elimelech would be lifted up."

"A child most worthy."

***

Though mid-Nison air blew cold from the northern

mountains, Ruth crouched beside a pail of seeds for the kitchen garden, wiping sweat from her brow. An ache in her back sharpened. She rubbed against it as best she could reach, but the ache rumbled around to the front, and sharp pain made her gasp.

Naomi flew to her feet. "Are you well? Has your time come?"

Ruth breathed against the pain. "We should finish the planting."

Naomi shook her head. "The child does not need to be birthed in dirt." She reached a hand for Ruth. "Come. I will send Serena to gather the women."

Not an hour had passed when Ruth found herself surrounded by women of Bethlehem as she lay panting after a deep pang of labor. Akiva, Zirre, and Serena she recognized, but there were others. Some gripped her hand as waves of pain rolled through. Others lifted their voices with her as she cried out. Cool water bathed her head. Labor moved quickly. She leaned up against her legs and pushed. Voices rose with excitement as the baby showed itself. Moments later, she fell back, exhausted. Gentle hands laid her on the pillow. The wail of a newborn erupted through the room. Women laughed and cried.

Naomi brushed Ruth's hair from her face and wiped at the sweat with a damp cloth. "A son. A fine son. Oh, my daughter, what joy you have given me."

Zirre drew close to them both. "Blessed be the Lord. He brought you a redeemer. May the name Boaz be renowned in Israel."

Akiva held the baby as an elder woman wrapped him in swaddling clothes. When he was laid upon Ruth, the women gathered around. "He is strong. Ethan is a good name for him."

"He is a gift of YHWH. His name should be Avishai."

Zirre places her hand on the back of the baby as Ruth stroked his cheek. Zirre smiled at the others. "He is here because both Lord Boaz and Ruth have hearts for serving and helping others."

The elder woman nodded. "Then his name should be Obed." The baby gurgled in the silence, then all laughed.

Naomi drew him to her. "Welcome, Obed, my son."

Zirre hugged them both. "He will be a restorer of your life. Someone to nurture through your old age. Your beloved daughter-in-law has born him. She has been better to you than seven sons."

Ruth watched her son as other women cared for her needs.

***

Boaz wondered at the flickering lights in the lower windows. It wasn't until after he'd given his horse to its keeper that the sound of a baby sang across the courtyard. Naomi held a bundle close. She lifted a finger to her lip. Boaz glanced at Ruth. Her cheeks were pale, and the lashes of her closed eyes looked like smudges on her skin. Naomi came to Boaz.

Wonder filled him as he took hold of the bundle, moving the blanket to reveal a perfect-formed face. The baby was tiny, and yet Boaz could feel the breath of his son.

Naomi sighed, her face bright with joy. "The women named him Obed. May he be as good a servant to others as you and Ruth have been."

Boaz blinked against tears in his eyes. "He's beautiful. YHWH be praised."

Naomi scooted past them. "Sit with him. I will prepare a light meal. Ruth needs to regain her strength and provide nourishment for the baby."

Watching his steps with care, he crossed the room to the bench beside his sleeping wife. All his years, he'd seen many children born, yet none as precious as the one he held in his arms. What joy they would have together. For now, he was content to watch over Ruth as he held his son, Obed.

Laurie Boulden is Assistant Professor of Elementary Education at Warner University. She volunteers time with youth and ladies' ministries at Trinity Baptist Church. She is a member of Word Weavers International and has attended the Florida Christian Writers Conference five years. She has won awards multiple years in the novel category for Biblical fiction, fantasy and science fiction, and contemporary romance. She won Writer of the Year in 2016. She recently completed a Master of Art in Creative Writing and English. Her interests lie in writing as well as teaching others to write. A good story deserves a good telling.

Other books by Laurie:

Jewel of Jericho
Hidden Gems
Cookies, Cocoa, and Capers